# "I'm Proposing A Marriage Of Convenience,"

Main said in a deep, low voice.

"A marriage of convenience for *whom?*" Stacy shot back with sarcastic skepticism.

"For us both, Stace. That's the beauty of an arranged marriage—I won't expect you to answer to me for every decision you make, and you won't expect mushy, meaningless words of undying love from me. We'll be equal partners, not only in the ranch operation, but in life, as well."

"I see. But what exactly would *my* contribution be to this business and lifetime partnership?"

Now Main paused. He took a long swallow of his beer, then drew a deep breath. "Children, for one thing."

"Children! You mean you'd expect . . ." Stacy's voice dried up, and she swallowed with visible difficulty.

"Of course," Main said with a sexy drawl. "I expect you to share my bed. . . ."

Dear Reader,

Joan Hohl is back! And I know you're all cheering at her return. Her *Man of the Month* book, *Convenient Husband,* is Joan at her steamiest, and her hero, Jasper (also known as "Main") Chance, is a man to remember. That's *all* I'm going to tell you about this sexy, sensuous story.... You'll just have to read it for yourself.

A book by Lass Small is always a treat, and you'll all be thrilled to know that *A Restless Man* is the first in her three-book series about those Fabulous Brown Brothers. (Yes, you first met Bob Brown in her 1991 *Man of the Month* book, *'Twas the Night.*) Look for more of the Brown men in October and December.

August is completed with a terrific story from Mary Lynn Baxter, *And Baby Makes Perfect* (another hero to remember!); *Just Like Old Times* by Jennifer Greene (watch out for the matchmaking teenagers!); *Midsummer Madness* by Christine Rimmer (with Cody McIntyre, town hunk); and *Sarah and the Stranger* by Shawna Delacorte, a new author you'll hear more of.

Next month, look for Silhouette Desire books by some of your favorite authors, including Annette Broadrick, Diana Palmer and Helen R. Myers.

All the best,

Lucia Macro
Senior Editor

# JOAN HOHL
## CONVENIENT HUSBAND

SILHOUETTE *Desire*®

Published by Silhouette Books New York

**America's Publisher of Contemporary Romance**

For Stacy Hauk, for her help and assistance.
Thanks, kid.

SILHOUETTE BOOKS
300 East 42nd St., New York, N.Y. 10017

CONVENIENT HUSBAND

ISBN: 0-373-05732-6

First Silhouette Books printing August 1992

Printed in the U.S.A.

## *JOAN HOHL*,

a Gemini and inveterate daydreamer, says she always has her head in the clouds. An avid reader all her life, she discovered romances about ten years ago. "And as soon as I read one," she confesses, "I was hooked." Now an extremely prolific author, she is thrilled to be getting paid for doing exactly what she loves best.

Wanner Family recipe compliments of my sister-in-law's mother, Laure (Wanner) Leininger. Thanks, Dee Dee.

## Raisin Pie (Funeral Pie)

**PIE CRUST:**

Either 9″ homemade pie crust or 9″ ready-made.

**PIE FILLING:**

*1 10 oz box raisins*
*1 cup water*
*½ cup brown sugar*
*1½ tbs vinegar*
*a dash of nutmeg*
*1 tbs cornstarch*

Combine raisins and water in a saucepan. Bring to boil, then reduce heat and simmer until fruit is softened and plump. Remove from heat and stir in remaining ingredients. Set aside to cool.

**CRUMB TOPPING:**

*1 tsp baking powder*
*1 cup flour*
*¾ cup sugar*
*2 tbs butter*
*1 egg, well beaten*
*½ cup milk*

Combine dry ingredients. Cut in butter until mixture is crumbly. Set aside ½ cup. Blend egg and milk into remaining crumb mixture.

Pour cooled pie filling into a pastry-lined 9″ pie pan, then pour egg-and-milk-crumb mixture over pie filling. Sprinkle ½ cup reserved crumb mixture over top. Bake at 450° for 10 minutes. Reduce heat to 350° and continue baking for another 25 minutes. Enjoy!

# One

Blue Ball.

Intercourse.

Paradise!

"Ha—I love it!" Jasper Chance hooted out loud, filling the interior of the rental car with the sound of his laughter. The force of his breath rattled the road map he'd spread out across the steering wheel.

His laughter subsiding to a chuckle, Jasper—known as Main to his friends—moved his long index finger over the map. His intent gaze followed the trail of his finger, searching for more interesting place names.

From the time he had learned to read, Main had been fascinated by the exotic- and unusual-sounding names of places and things. Intriguing names like: Baton Rouge, Jackson Hole, Andalusia, Taos; exotic-sounding things such as djellaba, pemmican, kayak, etc.

Jasper, the boy, would roll the strange names around inside his mind, savoring the images of excitement and adventure they conjured in his fertile imagination.

Main, the man, still did, and these particular place-names of towns and villages located in what was known as the Dutch Country of southeastern Pennsylvania were a kick for Main, a pure delight.

"E-phra-ta." Main sounded out the word, recalling it from the memory of hearing his mother read from the Bible. "Lit-itz...hmm," he murmured, pursing his lips. "Interesting. I'll have to check out a couple of these places." His lips smoothed into a wry smile. "That is, after I've checked out Miss Stacy Hunsberger."

Flattening one palm on the map, Main groped around for the slip of paper that had become wedged between the driver's seat and the console. Flipping open the folded sheet, he scanned the concise directions the lawyer's clip-voiced, starchy secretary had typed for him.

Frowning in concentration, he shifted his eyes from the directions to the map. The Philadelphia lawyer— one rather pompous and pedantic stick by name of Clarence Ridgeway Farraday, the Third, no less—had indicated in an insulting if oblique manner, that the most dim-witted of idiots should have little difficulty in locating the property in question. The man hadn't exactly endeared himself to Main with his supercilious, condescending attitude.

Being the possessor of a doctorate, as well as an M.B.A.—which he had acquired with minimal intellectual effort—Jasper was far removed from dimwitted idiocy.

"If I can find my way around the mountains in the Big Bend without getting myself lost," he muttered, peering at the map, "I can damn well locate a horse farm in a moderately populated section of Pennsylvania." A moment later, his finger stabbed at the paper and a grin slanted his mouth. "Ah-ha! Pay dirt!" he exclaimed, homing in on the desired area.

After glancing around to get his bearings and set his course, Main folded the map into its original position, fired the engine and drove off the soft shoulder and onto the two-lane blacktopped road.

As he tooled along the road behind a delivery van, a thought occurred that brought a grim smile to his lips.

"Ready or not, Miss Stacy Hunsberger," Jasper murmured, giving voice to his thought. "Here comes trouble, in the form of Main Chance."

"Do you really think that young woman is capable of handling Morning Star?"

Stacy looked up from the stream of water flowing over her hands to level a chiding smile at the man standing beside her at the sink. "That young woman's name is Anne, as you very well know," she said in mild reproof. "And I wouldn't have left her alone with my favorite horse if I didn't believe she was capable of handling the job of exercising her."

"But she's still new to the work, and Morning Star is a high-mettled Thoroughbred," the man said with dogged determination. "Leaving a novice alone with such an expensive animal is asking for trouble, if you ask me."

Suppressing an urge to point out the fact that she *hadn't* asked him, Stacy ripped a paper towel from the roll mounted on the wall above the sink, handed it to him, then ripped another one off for herself. She slid another glance at him while making a production out of drying her hands.

Daniel Slater was one of the local veterinarians. At thirty-three, Dan was mature, serious about life in general and his work in particular, attractive, personable and a proven good friend . . . sometimes too much of a good friend.

Stacy had known Dan most of her life; he and her older brother had been friends since kindergarten. When her brother had left home to attend a university in California and had decided to remain on the West Coast, Dan had stepped into the role of surrogate older brother and protector.

Stacy had a deep and genuine affection for Dan, but there were times when she felt constricted by his vigorous adherence to his adopted role.

This day, of all days, was proving to be one of those times. Stacy was emotionally uptight. She had a problem, a big problem, and Dan's overconcern about the capabilities, or lack thereof, of the new groom was beginning to work on her nerves, never mind her patience.

Responding to his comment with a reasonable facsimile of a careless shrug, Stacy turned away to lob the balled towel at the trash can positioned against the wall at the end of a row of cabinets. "Two off the back-board," she crowed as the paper ball bounced off the wall and into the can.

"You amaze me." Shaking his head, Dan walked to the can to deposit his crumpled towel. "I had half expected to find you ranting and raving, or at least grinding your teeth, when I arrived today."

"You expected me to rant and rave because one of my horses has colic?"

"No, of course not." Dan gave her an impatient look.

"You've lost me, Dan." Stacy's sigh reflected her own growing impatience. "What are you talking about?"

"Wasn't that man supposed to arrive today?"

"Ahh." Stacy sighed again. The expected arrival of "that man" was the reason she was so uptight. "Yes, that lawyer, Mr. Farraday, said he would very likely arrive today."

"Name's Chance, isn't it?"

"Yes, Jasper Chance." Stacy swallowed yet another sigh; she didn't want to think about Jasper Chance, the heretofore never-heard-of, far, far distant relative laying claim to half the inheritance that was rightfully hers.

"Well?"

"Well...what?" Stacy kept her expression bland; Dan wasn't fooled or impressed.

"Come on, Stace," he said chidingly. "Remember me? I know you. You've got a short fuse and a long temper." His smile was tender. "And you're too composed. You make me feel like I'm walking through a mine field.''

"Got you on tippy-toes, do I?'' Stacy laughed, and felt a slight easing of the tension crawling along her nerves. "Well, you can relax. I'm not going to explode all over you. What good would ranting, raving and grinding my teeth do me?'' she asked, crossing the spotless tile kitchen floor to the fridge. "Want a cola or iced tea?''

"Tea, please, no sugar.'' Dan frowned. "You've been pretty tense since you received notification of this man's claim,'' he said. "Maybe an outburst of emotion might ease the strain a bit.''

"When and if this person arrives,'' Stacy said, smiling grimly, "a right to the jaw might relieve a lot more tension, and be a lot more satisfying.'' Swinging open the fridge door, she withdrew from the top shelf a pitcher filled with tea and carried it to the countertop. "Then again,'' she mused, absently removing two tall glasses from the cabinet above the counter, "I believe a load of buckshot to his rump just might dissolve the tension entirely.''

"Stacy!''

Dan's outcry shattered her reverie. Jolting, Stacy spun to face him, sugar spoon in hand. "What?'' Alert, adrenaline pumping into her system, she skimmed a sharp-eyed look around the room expecting ... who knew what? "What's wrong?''

"You put sugar in my tea!'' he accused, obviously fighting a bout of laughter. "I'd rather you ranted, raved and blew off some steam.''

"Sugar?" Quivering with reaction and a sense of letdown, Stacy stared at him in blank amazement. "You nearly scared me into a heart attack, and all because of a couple of teaspoons of sugar?"

"No, not because of the sugar." Dan frowned. "The sugar is beside the point."

"I'll say," Stacy muttered, turning to dump the tea into the sink. "What is the point?"

"You, and your obvious state of distraction." He came to stand beside her at the counter, sliding one arm around her waist. "And you need your wits about you to work with horses. Besides, what good is all this tension doing you? If this man does indeed have a legitimate claim, I really don't think there is very much you can do about it."

"Oh, no?" Stacy spun inside his encircling arm to stare at him in challenge. "If you think for one minute that I would give up this farm, *my* farm, without a fight...a real nasty, back-to-the-wall fight, you can think again." Her normally placid hazel eyes glittered with sparks of anger. "This farm and everything on it is mine," she said, her voice harsh with strain. "And you can bet your...er...whatever, that I intend to hang on to it, and as sole owner."

"But how?" Dan arched his light brown eyebrows. "If his claim to a half interest in the property is legitimate, I don't see how you'd have a legal leg to stand on."

"But his claim can't be legitimate!" Stacy exclaimed. "I'm sure there must be some sort of mistake." Distraught, feeling a need for physical action, she broke free of his loose hold. "I can't, won't believe that my grandfather added a codicil to his will shortly before he died, leaving a half interest in the farm to a stranger.''

"But your lawyer said . . ."

"That's another thing I don't understand.'' She interrupted him with a cry. "After using the same Lancaster law firm for as long as I can remember, why would my grandfather use a Philadelphia lawyer to add a codicil to his will?''

"Possibly because he didn't want to explain his reason for adding the codicil,'' Dan said, guessing.

Agitated, Stacy raked her fingers through the strands of chestnut hair smoothed to her head, dislodging the clip anchoring the long mass at her nape. "But it doesn't make sense. The will has already gone into probate.'' She shook her head, loosening her hair even more. "Then, out of the blue comes this letter from this lawyer, Mr. Farraday, informing my lawyer, Mr. Knowles, of the codicil my grandfather supposedly added to his will. And dammit, I don't believe it!''

"What I still don't quite understand,'' Dan said, frowning, "is how this Mr. Farraday learned about your grandfather's death.''

"That's the part that really bites,'' Stacy said through her teeth. "I notified him.''

"What?'' Dan's expression went blank. "How?''

Stacy sighed and gave him a helpless look. "While I was going through Gramp's papers, I found a letter, sealed and stamped, addressed simply to Mr. Farraday in Philadelphia.'' Her shoulders lifted and fell. "Clipped to the letter was a note, written in my grandfather's hand, with the instruction that the letter be mailed in the event of his death." A self-mocking smile curved her lips. "I mailed it."

"Which is why the codicil took so long to come to light," Dan concluded.

"Yes."

"Which also proves my theory that your grandfather chose an out-of-town lawyer because he didn't want to explain his reasons for adding the codicil."

"But Gramps always said the farm was to come to me," Stacy argued, moving away to pace the floor. "He wanted me to have it because he knew I loved it as much as he did." The resounding thud of her low-heeled work boots as she restlessly paced the floor punctuated her terse voice.

"I know." Dan nodded. "But I also know he wanted to see you settled into marriage, protected by a husband."

The look Stacy tossed at him over her rigid shoulder might have stopped traffic. "Marriage!" she yelped. "What does marriage have to do with this?"

Dan shrugged. "It's just a wild thought, but I bet that's why your grandfather changed his mind, and his will...to force your hand."

Stacy raised her eyes, as if seeking help from above. "Dan, really, how in heaven's name would my having to share the farm with a stranger force me into marriage?"

"For moral support, or even for financial assistance to buy out the claimant's interest," Dan replied evenly, overlooking the sarcasm lacing her voice. "You've admitted that you're almost broke since paying off the outstanding debts and inheritance taxes."

"Not almost," she muttered. "I'm completely broke. I've got barely enough to get by."

"And I'm suggesting that your grandfather knew to the penny what your financial situation would be." Dan's smile contained both understanding and commiseration. "Where else would you get the money to buy out the claimant? From a bank?" He shook his head. "Old Jacob knew you too well. You'd mortgage your soul—or your freedom—before you mortgaged this farm."

An expression of numbed shock filling her face, Stacy came to a shuddering halt. "He wouldn't," she said in a strained whisper. "My gramps wouldn't do a thing like that to me." Her eyes had a pleading look. "Would he?"

"Yes, I'm afraid I believe he would." Dan's voice was gentle but adamant. "Jacob was a determined old man, dead set on having his way."

Stacy wanted to argue, longed to deny Dan's analysis of her beloved grandfather, but in all honesty she could not; Dan's description of the crusty old man was right on target. Jacob Hunsberger had always been a determined man, set on having his own way, and he had made no bones or excuses about it. And, especially during the last year of his life, Jacob had been unrelenting in his desire to see Stacy securely tied in wedlock.

Stacy had loved the old man deeply. She had trusted him unconditionally. Jacob's eleventh-hour betrayal was like a knife thrust to the heart.

Although Stacy concealed the wound behind a mask of self confidence, inside she felt mortally injured. But since she couldn't bring herself to the point of resenting the much-loved man responsible for her present dilemma, she centered her resentment on the distant and unknown relative her grandfather had designated as her coheir.

Her gentle eyes narrowed, her soft mouth set in a hard, mutinous line, Stacy stared into Dan's compassion-softened expression.

"You think I'm right," he murmured, walking to her to clasp her hands in a gesture of support. "Don't you?"

"I'm *afraid* you're right," Stacy admitted, though it cost her dearly to do so. "Gramps was hell-bent on seeing me shackled." She heaved a sigh, then gave him a crooked smile. "You've got some money, Dan," she said in a forced teasing tone. "Do you want to marry me?"

"No," he replied with soft but blunt honesty. "But I will . . . if that's what you want."

Stacy squeezed his hands in appreciation, while shaking her head in denial. "Thanks...but no thanks. You know as well as Gramps did how I feel about marriage."

Dan smiled. "If I recall correctly, I believe *bondage* was the word you used to describe the institution."

"Precisely." Stacy didn't return the smile. Her soft mouth tightened into a hard straight line. "I've seen what marriage does to most women."

"What does it do?" Dan raised one eyebrow. "I mean, other than give them financial security?"

"Financial security? Ha!" Stacy sneered. "Do you, as a mere man, have any idea what price women pay for that dubious illusion you call financial security?"

Accustomed to Stacy's occasional feminist outbursts, Dan's lips twitched with amusement, but he did manage a serious tone of voice. "Price? No...but somehow I have a feeling you'll be happy to educate me, a mere man, on the subject. What price do women pay for security?"

"In-de-pen-dence," she elucidated, pronouncing each syllable distinctly.

"Ah, c'mon, Stace," he protested.

"C'mon nothing!" Stacy planted her hands on her slender hips and scowled at him. "Most of the friends I grew up with, went to college with, are now married, and the *majority* of them—even the ones who earn more money than their husbands—enjoy precious little independence or autonomy. From what I have observed, and I've looked long and close, married life for the modern, liberated woman of today isn't all that much different than what it ever was. Drudgery." Her lip curled. "Dinner must be on the table by a certain time...*his* time. The home must be spotless at all times, the laundry done...by *her,* in most cases. And, if there are children, well, of course, that is primarily *her* department." She actually snorted. "Give me a break. If that's marriage . . . I'll take vanilla."

"I disagree."

"Too bad." Stacy had the look of a she-wolf protecting her territory.

Dan shrugged his shoulders in a sign of surrender. "Okay, wedded bliss is out."

"Believe it."

Concern shadowed the amusement in Dan's eyes. "So, if the man's claim is just, as I suspect it is, mortgaging the farm is unacceptable and a marriage of convenience is out of the question...."

"It is." She broke in to reinforce her position.

"Then, other than to come up with the money to buy him out, there is really nothing you can do about it, is there?"

"Wrong." Stacy's smile was serene ... and chilling. "I can make his life a living hell."

# Two

___

His dark eyes alight with fascination and amusement, Main drove along the narrow secondary road at a snail's pace, set by a horse-drawn buggy in front of him. It was the second such vehicle he had seen since exiting the Pennsylvania Turnpike, but the first one he had had an opportunity to view up close. The two buggies looked exactly alike, being boxlike in design and all in unrelieved black.

Main got a good look at the buggy driver when he made a right turn at intersecting roads and, like the conveyance, the man was attired in black, even to the full beard concealing the lower half of his face.

"Fascinating," he murmured, curiously studying the somberly dressed older gentleman.

Was the man one of the Plain People he had read about? Main mused. Amish? Mennonite? How did one tell the difference between the two sects? His train of thought produced a new and startling consideration. For all Main knew, Stacy Hunsberger might well be a member of one of the sects. And, if she was, would it make any difference to the outcome of their meeting? he pondered, waiting patiently for a slow-moving car to pull out in front of him from the bisecting road.

Well, he'd soon find out, Main decided, a frown creasing his brow as he eased along behind the car ahead of him. Was driving at a near crawl the norm in this part of the country? he wondered, tamping down a flash of irritation. Accustomed to driving at speed in the sparsely populated, desolate regions of West Texas, the sedate pace imposed on him by the driver ahead was beginning to get to him.

A curse sprang to Main's tight lips when the car in front of him reduced speed even more, but changed to a sigh of relief when the turning signal flashed on. Keeping a tight rein on his temper, Main brought the car to a stop. Drumming his fingertips against the steering wheel while he waited for the vehicle to inch its way onto a private road, he glanced around in search of diversion. Bored, edgy, he focused his attention on a rectangular sign fastened to the split-rail property fence.

A wry smile eased the tightness of Main's lips as he read the two words printed in black on the small, simple white sign. Hunsberger Farm. He had reached his destination but, had it not been for the slowness of the driver in front of him, he'd have driven past it without notice.

His attention centered, Main ran a sharp-eyed look over the fence. Even with his limited view, he noted several rails and a post that needed replacing. He frowned, wondering if the disrepair was due to lack of interest or lack of funds. Reserving judgment until he had more facts, Main set the car in motion and drove onto the private road.

A few yards inside the entrance, he brought the car to a stop once more. The other slow-moving car had disappeared around a curve in the narrow road. Pushing open his door, Main stepped out onto the spall-covered dirt road. Squinting against the glare of bright afternoon sunshine, he stared in the direction in which the other vehicle had gone.

An abundance of trees, in full spring-green leaf, obscured Main's vision, but in the distance he could make out the rooftops of several buildings.

The split-rail fence ran parallel to the road on either side, enclosing verdant pastures and the horses grazing within them. The scene was soothing and alluring. The soft air was redolent with the earthy scent of spring.

"Beautiful." He spoke his thought aloud. "Absolutely beautiful."

Main drew a deep breath, then leaving the car door hanging open, he walked to the fence. Resting his arms on the upper rail, and bracing one foot on the lowest rail, he gazed entranced at the pastoral panorama spread out before him.

Without doubt, this gently rolling countryside was some of the most beautiful that Main had ever seen. Green. Everything was so lush and green. The complete opposite of the dry, desolate terrain of West Texas.

The fresh, sweet-smelling air caressed his skin and ruffled his longish hair. Main smiled, and unfastened the buttons on his shirt to give the breeze access to more of his sun-warmed flesh.

An unexpected feeling of tranquility permeated his being. Time lost all meaning. For now, for this instant, Main was content to bask in the sunlight and reflect on the long, winding path that had led him to this special place. . . .

Main's life path had its beginning at his birthplace in Tyler, Texas. Yet, from an early age, he had felt an inner urge, a siren whisper to be . . . somewhere else. He didn't have a clue as to where that somewhere else was located, or even if it existed outside the inner longing, but he had spent the majority of his adult life searching for the elusive place.

Undefined, unspecified, but always there, hovering at the edge of his mind, the yearning to be elsewhere remained within Main as he strode along his life path.

The first stride took Main from Texas to a university in the Midwest and, although he liked the locale and the people he came in contact with, the area didn't satisfy the hollow spot deep inside him.

After graduate school, Main accepted a position with a small but prestigious brokerage firm in Chicago. He found the business of investments mentally stimulating, and the city of Chicago interesting and invigorating, but neither the work nor the environment were equal to the ever-expanding inner compulsion to be ... somewhere, the somewhere he instinctively felt he should be, where he belonged.

From Chicago, Main's meandering path led him to Wall Street in New York City, and to a position with a much larger and even more prestigious brokerage firm. His work there was exciting, financially rewarding and physically taxing.

Within weeks after his arrival in New York, Main was introduced to a small, stunning, raven-haired beauty who was also pursuing a career in the investment field. The attraction, physical and professional, between them was immediate and strong and, within a month of their first meeting, they decided to share an apartment.

Neither he nor the woman had deluded themselves, or each other, about being in love. There was a strong physical attraction ... period. With his experience, of life and women, Main wasn't sure he even believed in the vague, undefined emotion called romantic love.

The life-style Main subsequently acquired bordered on frenetic. For a time, the deep-seated inner urge to be elsewhere was smothered by the increasing demands of his daily routine, and the euphoric aftermath of his nightly satiation.

The sex was great ... for a time, and being normal, healthy and all male, Main steeped himself in the charms of his willing and imaginative partner.

But the pace was killing. Being young and ambitious, Main ignored the early telltale signs of physical wear and tear and psychological damage.

Main was playing a game, an exciting game of buying and selling. He was making an unbelievable amount of money, so much money that, before long, the money itself lost its value; it was the game that was important, not the reward.

Main's first inkling of the results of the breakneck pace he was maintaining came with the realization of the dissipation of his desire for his live-in lover. His lack of sexual interest didn't bother him at first, since he had recently concluded that they had very little in common other than their initial mutual physical attraction and their dedication to their respective careers. Deciding the newness and excitement of their relationship had worn off, Main shrugged aside his concern over the apparent dwindling of his sex drive.

But Main's second inkling was not as easily shrugged aside. That inkling came soon after he and his live-in agreed to part. There were no scenes, no recriminations. She moved out. He was free, and since he had chosen to remain faithful to her while they were together, that freedom justified his right to choose another bed partner.

Intent on exercising his new freedom, Main accepted an invitation to a private party at the uptown home of a business associate. Due to a late meeting in connection to a potentially large transaction he was working on, the party was in full swing by the time Main arrived at the town house.

The party atmosphere was loose—to say the least. There appeared to be a seemingly endless supply of food, drinks and readily available women. Main had barely set foot inside the house when the realization hit him that he simply was not interested—not in the food, not in the booze, not even in the prospect of female companionship.

Telling himself he was merely tired, and fully aware that he would never be missed, either by his host or any of the guests, Main left the party and went home—alone.

Main remained alone—as far as female companionship went—for a long period after the night of the party. He was busy, much too busy to take the time and effort necessary to begin a new relationship or even a brief involvement. At least, that was what he told himself. Main was also tired, and growing more tired with each successive day.

It was about a month later that the inkling nagging at Main expanded into sharp and startling self-acknowledgment. The insight struck him one morning with the shrill summons of his bedside alarm. Instead of hitting the floor running, as he always had, Main muttered a curse against yet another early morning appointment, shut off the alarm, shifted into a more comfortable position and promptly fell back to sleep.

When Main finally awoke near noon, he acknowledged the need to rethink his life-style. He was more than merely tired, and he knew it. He was burning out. The pace he had been keeping was taking its toll on his body and his mind. And, though it was true that he was making a lot of money, he was beginning to question the financial value in relation to the cost.

The phone rang. Main ignored it. He consequentially ignored the trill of the phone throughout that day. He had some serious thinking to do, some important decisions to make.

In the end, Main found it surprisingly easy to reach and execute his decision. He had had it. After tying up as many professional loose ends as he possibly could, he quit his job and, a few weeks later, the city.

From New York, Main's life path led him to West Texas, and a completely opposite life-style. While Main enjoyed the laid-back, unpressured pace of West Texas, with more time to reflect, get in tune with his feelings, he became aware once again of an inner urge to be elsewhere.

Main was puzzling over where, exactly, that elsewhere might be, when he received the letter from the Philadelphia lawyer, informing him of his inheritance of half interest in the horse farm in Pennsylvania where his grandmother had been raised. Even now, Main wasn't sure which of the two bits of information surprised him most—the fact that he had apparently inherited a half interest in a horse farm, or the more startling fact that his grandmother apparently had grown up on the property. Main had always believed that his grandmother, like his grandfather, was a Tyler, Texas, native....

A loud nicker from one of the horses inside the pasture penetrated the memory fog clouding Main's mind, ending his reverie. He expelled a long breath as he straightened away from the fence. The day was wearing on, and he had an appointment to keep—an appointment that had taken on a lot more importance within the past few minutes.

Main retraced his steps to the car, then turned to sweep the landscape with a narrowed, contemplative gaze.

Oh, yeah, he thought, bringing his gaze to rest on the sleek animals in the pasture. His forthcoming appointment with Stacy Hunsberger had taken on infinitely more importance for the simple if somewhat confusing fact that, suddenly but definitely, Main knew that he had found his elusive somewhere.

This gently rolling, lush green countryside was the somewhere he had been searching for all of his adult life. It was his. Main knew it, felt it to the marrow of his bones.

But there was another who claimed ownership to this sweet piece of property. Main had a deep-in-the-gut instinct that his meeting with Stacy Hunsberger was going to come down to a clash of wills.

A dry, grim smile crept along Main's taut lip line. If it came to a fight, Miss Stacy would find herself in the battle of her life. And she would lose, because Main knew that he couldn't allow anything or anybody to eject him from this place. It was as basic as that.

Jasper Chance had come home.

Mentally and physically prepared for whatever had to be faced, Main slid behind the wheel and set the car in motion. The farmhouse and outbuildings came into view after he rounded the bend in the road. The sight of them strengthened his certainty. It was weird, creepy, almost scary, but there it was: he belonged here.

The house had a deep front porch, and as he drove closer, Main could see three people standing at the top of the steps leading up to the porch. There was a man and two women, one young and slim, the other older, matronly in appearance.

Main surmised that one of the women was his adversary. But which one? he asked himself, bringing the car to a stop at the base of the porch steps.

The older of the two was plump, round-faced with ruddy cheeks and pleasant looking. The younger woman was taller, slender yet gently rounded, with hair the exact same shade as the chestnut Thoroughbred he'd taken particular note of in the pasture. She was not beautiful, but...

Main felt a strange contraction of pain in his chest, and a tightening in another part of his body. A fleeting thought shot through his mind as he pushed open the car door and stepped onto the graveled road.

*God! Fighting with the redhead could prove to be fun.*

# Three

---

"Mr. Chance?" Stacy started down the porch steps, hand extended, as the stranger exited the car.

"Yes." The man slammed the door, circled the car, and reaching out, grasped her hand in a firm clasp, while offering a tentative smile. "Miss Hunsberger?"

"Yes," Stacy responded, praying her expression reflected her calm tone of voice and not her reaction to the look of the man.

To say her reaction to his appearance was negative, would have been the height of understatement. Aversion came closer to the mark. His crisp-looking pin-striped shirt was open to his narrow, belted waist, revealing a flatly muscled chest matted by a diamond-shaped cloud of tightly curled dark hair.

Since reaching an age to notice such things, Stacy had never been turned on by the sight of a manly chest covered by hair; she was equally unappreciative of the type of male who displayed his hair-swathed pectorals by leaving his shirt undone.

Still, in all fairness, Stacy had to concede to the fact of the man's undeniable attractiveness; for in truth, Jasper Chance was a good-looking man.

His muscularly lean body towered some six or so inches over her own five-foot-seven-inch frame. His facial features were sharply defined—cheekbones high, jaw firm, nose longish but straight. Thin masculine lips parted to reveal strong teeth, flashing white in contrast to his sun-burnished skin. A shock of unruly hair the rich brown color of cured tobacco, also a trifle longish but styled by an obvious expert, gleamed with a healthy sheen in the bright spring sunshine. But, by far, the most imposing of his features were his eyes; framed by ridiculously long lashes, his gray eyes were alert, sharp and possessed the piercing quality of a laser—or a bird of prey.

His incisive stare, his firm hand clasp, the very look of him made Stacy nervous, which, in turn, undermined her sense of purpose, while abrading her feelings of resentment and anger toward him.

Stacy disliked the man at once. At the same time, she was forced to quash an urge to smooth her disheveled hair and neatly tuck her blouse into her jeans.

Her inner contradictory reaction to him set a spark to Stacy's temper. She met his riveting stare, her hazel eyes glittering with the light of renewed purpose and determination.

"Have I arrived at an inopportune moment?" Releasing her hand, and the visual hammerlock he had on her eyes, Jasper Chance glanced around at the two others present, one eyebrow quirking as he noted their expressions of blatant curiosity and interest in the meeting.

His voice was low, deep, rich, soothing. Stacy was anything but soothed. She bristled at the sound of it, and at the strange and unwelcome sensation of sudden coolness in the palm of her now-empty right hand. Choosing prudence over honesty, she refrained from informing him that his arrival at *any* time would have been inopportune.

"Not at all." Her brisk tone of voice belied her assertion. She turned to smile at Dan and the older woman. "My housekeeper has just returned..." Her voice trailed away as Jasper Chance strode forward, hand extended to the woman. The warm, friendly smile on his face caused a twinge of unease in Stacy's chest. She disregarded the odd feeling and the sudden catch in her voice as she made the proper introduction.

"Edith, this is Mr. Jasper Chance. Mr. Chance, my housekeeper, Edith Fromm."

"My pleasure," Jasper Chance said, wrapping his long-fingered hand around hers. His smile beguiling, he raised his arched brows. "Mrs.—Miss—Fromm?"

"Mrs." The charmed expression on Edith's apple-cheeked face made Stacy cringe. "I'm pleased to make your acquaintance, Mr. Chance." Her smile was close to girlish. "And I'm just plain Edith to everyone around here."

"Nothing plain about you, Edith," Jasper Chance said with smooth gallantry. "And, to every one of my friends in West Texas, I'm known as Main."

"Main?"

Stacy and Edith spoke in unison, and stared at him with reflecting frowns of incomprehension. But before Jasper Chance could reply, Dan clarified their confusion with two softly spoken words.

"Main Chance."

Main shifted his laser stare to the other, younger man. "Exactly." A wry grin ambled across his lips. "I am blessed with friends who all possess a weird sense of humor."

Dan returned the grin. "Sounds like fun to me." Stepping forward, he offered his hand. "I'm Daniel Slater, one of the local vets," he explained, gripping Main's hand. "My friends call me Dan." He shot a teasing glance at Stacy. "I'm afraid that my friends share a rather prosaic sense of humor."

"Dan!" Stacy exclaimed in protest, ignoring the unmistakable sound of a chuckle from Edith.

"Too bad, Slater," Main murmured in solemn tones belied by his widening grin. "If my friends were your friends, they likely would have dubbed you Slate."

"It would have fit, too. Especially as archaically defined as harshly critical."

Everyone turned in startled surprise to the caustic tone of the new voice.

"Well, hello, another country heard from," Main drawled, obviously amused. "A well educated one at that." Once again, he offered his hand, and a smile, in greeting. "Name's Jasper Chance," he said, running a quick, appreciative glance over the young woman's slender form. "But you may call me Main."

"You already consider me a friend?" she inquired in a dust-dry tone, revealing that she had overheard most of the conversation.

"You remind me of a friend," Main countered, skimming another glance over her. "Like you, she is small and deceptively fragile looking. Her name's Selena."

"That's a beautiful name."

"For a beautiful woman." Main smiled. "What's yours?"

"I'm Anne Kulp," she said, gripping his proffered hand. An impish smile tilted her lips. "And I don't particularly care what my friends call me."

"You're a relative?" Main shot a sharp-eyed glance from Anne to Stacy.

"No," Stacy answered.

"I'm the new groom," Anne replied simultaneously.

"Why did you leave Morning Star?" Dan inserted in a harsh-voiced demand.

Anne gave him a dismissive look. "Morning Star is fine. The bout of colic is over."

"You have a horse with colic?" Although Main directed the question to Stacy, Dan answered.

"Yes." Dan glowered at Anne. "And I think I'd better have a look at her, just to make certain it has passed."

"Darn it, Slater, I know—" Anne began in protest, only to break off as, ignoring her, Dan muttered something under his breath about untrained, flighty young females, and strode off toward the stables.

"Wait, Dan. I'll go with you," Stacy called, rushing off after him.

Anne shook her head. "I guess I'd better go, too," she said, sighing as she turned to follow the other two.

"And I'd better see to getting lunch," Edith announced. The sound of the screen door banging shut behind her reverberated on the mild spring air.

His expression sanguine, Main stood at ease in the suddenly deserted yard. "Welcome to the farm, Chance," he murmured, drolly. "But why didn't that Philadelphia lawyer tell me it was the funny farm?"

Shrugging, Main slid his hands into his pants pockets and sauntered along the path taken by the others.

Interesting, he mused, glancing around as he meandered toward the stables, mentally commenting not on the property, but about the humans on it.

And, as far as the humans were concerned, there was certainly a fascinating combination of characteristics here. Of course, of primary interest to Main was his coheir.

Stacy Hunsberger resented him.

No surprise there; he had expected her resentment. A wry smile quirked Main's lips. What he hadn't expected was the impact on his body and senses at the sight of her.

Odd, he thought, pausing to consider his extraordinary reaction to Stacy. She was not at all his type.

Like a number of other tall men of his acquaintance, the type of women Main was usually attracted to were small, if not downright petite, slim to skinny, breath-catchingly beautiful, intelligent and vivacious.

Stacy was too tall, too curvy and, though striking in looks, not at all beautiful in a classic sense, and he suspected, much, much too feisty. As far as her intelligence went, the jury was still out on that particular attribute; he hadn't known her long enough to make a judgment.

So, in retrospect, Main reflected, why had he experienced such a strong and immediate attraction to her? A frown knit his brows and he stared into middle distance, contemplating his odd reaction to Stacy Hunsberger, the effects of which were still tingling not unpleasantly in the most vulnerable part of his body.

When no satisfactory answer sprang to mind, Main shoved the puzzling issue aside for future consideration and resumed walking at a leisurely pace.

Odd but interesting, he mused, as were the other characters in this situation.

Take Anne Kulp, for example.... A silent chuckle rose to Main's throat at the realization that in the not-too-distant past he would have been tempted to take whatever the lovely Anne might offer. To a greater extent than Stacy, Anne more closely fit the description of his type of woman. She was small, slender, with a mass of honey-blond hair framing a delicately featured, startlingly beautiful face. And Anne had certainly given the appearance of being vivacious.

Main chuckled aloud as he recalled Anne's flippant rejoinder to his comment about a nickname for Dan Slater.

Now there was another character in the drama in which Main found himself. At first, Dan Slater had appeared pleasant, easygoing, open. Yet he had shut down abruptly when Anne had arrived on the scene, becoming brusque and impatient.

One could almost smell the sulfur from the sparks Anne and Dan had struck off one another. A clash of personalities? A genuine dislike for each other? Main wondered. Or could there possibly be a deeper, intense if unacknowledged attraction between the two simmering beneath the surface?

Interesting indeed. Main concluded that even if he had no vested interest in the place, it would be worth hanging around, if only to watch the drama unfold.

But he did have an interest in the place, a half interest to be precise. Main skimmed another keen glance around the area, drinking into his senses the soft spring green, absorbing into his system the scent and feel of the landscape.

He belonged, whether or not Stacy Hunsberger believed it, agreed with it, liked it or...

Main's introspection was distracted by the approach of the woman he was thinking about. There was no sign of Anne Kulp, but Dan Slater was at Stacy's side. Their heads were lowered and they were so deep in conversation, they were unaware of Main's presence.

Observing the two, so obviously close in spirit as well as in body, Main experienced an unfamiliar but definite twinge of disquiet and anger.

Were Stacy and Dan more than friends? Were they, in fact, lovers? The thought created an image in Main's mind, an image so sexually explicit it was intolerable.

Confused and uncomfortable by the sudden rage of emotions churning inside his mind, Main stepped to the side to intercept, and subsequently, separate them. Knowing he had to say something, he said the first thing that sprang to mind.

"Is the animal all right?"

# Four

---

Stacy knew he was there, standing alongside the path to the stables, and yet the rough-edged sound of his voice startled her. She had been aware, much too much aware of him, his presence, from the instant he stepped out of the car.

The depth of her awareness of Jasper Chance annoyed Stacy in the extreme. Reacting to that annoyance, she raised her head, and as if he had just that moment materialized out of thin air, she stared at him in feigned, wide-eyed surprise.

"Oh, Mr. Chance! I . . . eh . . ."

"Forgot I was here?" He supplied the finish she seemed to be having trouble articulating.

Stacy moved her head and shoulders in a deliberately challenging and provoking manner. "Well, yes," she admitted in a bold-faced lie, turning to face him squarely. "As a matter of fact, in the confusion of the moment, I completely forgot that you were here."

His reaction to her show of unconcern, to her statement, was at once evident and intimidating. He smiled in a predatory way that drew goose bumps to the surface of her skin, and tangled his narrow-eyed gaze with hers.

"In that case, I suppose I'll have to work at making a stronger, more lasting impression on you," he murmured in a soft, suggestive growl. "Won't I?"

The intensity of his visual onslaught, in combination with the double meaning of his remark, was intellectually and physically stimulating and it played hell with Stacy's equilibrium. A barrage of strange and conflicting sensations of excitement and outrage stormed through her. Along with all the other emotions churning inside, she felt an urgent need to slap him—or at the very least, *verbally* slap him down.

Drawing her composure and wits together, Stacy maintained his stare with her own. "Oh, I really don't think that will be necessary." A taunting smile softened the tight lines of her mouth. "Chances are, Mr. Chance," she continued, mockingly, "I'll hazard a guess that you won't be here long enough to make any kind of lasting impression."

"Ah . . . Stace," Dan groaned.

Stacy responded to Dan with a silencing shrug, and continued to stare with blatant defiance at Jasper Chance. A shivery sense of unease crawled down her spine when he smiled, then laughed outright at her.

"Guess again," he drawled, matching her taunting tone. "I'm here, and I intend to stay here." He released his visual grip to sweep her form with a remote, dismissive glance. "My claim is legal, little girl."

Stacy had to restrain herself against flying at him, nails and teeth bared. At that moment, she wasn't even certain which of his taunts incensed her more, his stated intent of remaining on the farm, his boast about the legality of his claim, or his condescending use of the term "little girl."

"You…you son of a…" she began, sputtering, only to have her emotion-tight voice trail away when Dan stepped in front of her.

"Stop it, Stacy!" Though Dan's voice was soft, it contained an underlying note of command. "Name-calling will solve nothing. And that goes for you, too," he admonished Main. Moving to stand sideways between them, he glanced from one to the other. "You two have got to sit down together and sort this out."

To Stacy, his advice had the effect of a torch set to gasoline. She exploded. "Dammit, Dan, there's nothing to sort out! This farm is mine!"

"Wrong," Main retorted. "This farm is ours."

"Ours!" Stacy repeated, staring at him in angry astonishment. "Never!"

Displaying an arrogant disregard for Dan's blocking presence, Main moved around him, coming to a halt mere inches from Stacy. He raised a hand and snagged her chin with two fingers to tilt her face up to his.

"Never?" he taunted in a shiver-inducing whisper. "Oh, sweetheart, never say never."

His casual use of the endearment increased her anger to fury. Stacy wanted to retaliate, longed to lash out at him, backing him up, setting him down, but first and foremost move away from his stifling proximity. She wanted to, longed to, but the light pressure of his fingertips against the soft, vulnerable flesh on the underside of her chin was creating an adverse effect on her vocal chords.

A gentle, mind-seducing warmth spread in everwidening circles from his finger-point of contact, impeding thought, interfering with her breathing process, closing her throat to the voice of protest.

Feeling like a fish out of water, out of her element, out of her *league,* Stacy stared into his unreadable, emotion-darkened eyes, stunned speechless by the incredible and unbelievable sensations his touch had the power to inflict on her senses and nervous system.

It was not to be borne, and yet, for that instant of infinity, Stacy lacked the will, the impetus and the motor skills required to end the moment and the exquisite torture, by removing herself from his demoralizing touch by simply jerking her chin away from his fingers.

For Stacy, the experience was so new, so very unfamiliar, she was at a loss as to how to combat it. In effect, she was rendered helpless in the face of his effortless capture of her flesh, intellect and emotions.

What, if anything, Stacy could have done to terminate the moment, she was never to know, for Jasper Chance ended it himself by gliding his fingers to the very tip of her chin, then dropping his hand to his side.

Scarce seconds had elapsed in actual time of his control of her, and yet Stacy felt bereft, a sense of loss, chilled to the bone by the sudden denial of his warming touch.

But Stacy's senses and sense were restored, and with their restoration came a revitalizing resurgence of pride, anger and fierce defiance.

"How dare you presume to touch me?" she ground out in a harsh voice betraying strain.

"Touch you?" Main laughed, sparking pinpoints of lights of amusement in his eyes. "You call that brush of my fingers a touch?" He didn't wait for a response from her, but went on in a chiding tone, "That was nothing." The laughter fled from his eyes, replaced by an enticing, darkly sensuous gleam. "Believe me, if I ever touch you—*meaningfully* touch you—you will know, and appreciate, the difference."

His assurance—threat?—scored a direct hit to the very core of her being. Suppressing an urge to shiver, she stiffened her spine, squared her shoulders and injected an acid note of derision into her unsteady voice.

"Dream on, Texan." Stacy curled her quivering lips into a semblance of a sneer as she swept his tall, angular frame with a swift, dismissive glance. "You will never, and I repeat, *never* again get the opportunity to touch me—meaningfully or any other way," she avowed determinedly.

"Really?" Main's smile was loaded—with condescension, and all manner of sensual intent Stacy didn't care to speculate upon. But even if she had, he didn't allow her the time. "Let me offer you a piece of advice garnered from my broader experience of life, and the pitfalls inherent in the living of it," he went on smoothly. "And that is—always try to keep your words as sweet as possible because, chances are, you will likely end up having to eat at least eighty percent of them."

Stacy had heard enough, more than enough, and she had certainly had much more than enough of him. Suddenly, and with a gratifying sense of release, lashing out at him was easy.

"And you, Mr. Know-It-All-Texan, can take your broader experience advice and shove it, you...you..."

"I think this is about where I came in," Dan interjected, in a curious, muffled voice.

Stacy shot a sharp look at him to ascertain if he was choking back laughter, but Dan thwarted her by turning and striding off in the direction of the house.

"And this is where I make my exit," he called back over his shoulder, laughter now evident in his voice, "I'll stop by sometime tomorrow to check on Morning Star. Until then, have fun, but fight nice, you two."

"Fight nice. Have fun!" Had Dan slipped over the edge of reason? Stacy asked herself, staring after the vet in open-mouthed amazement. Then she heard the distinct sound of a soft, deep-throated chuckle from the man still standing too close to her for comfort. She whipped around to confront Jasper Chance just as a loud summons from Edith rang out on the spring breeze.

"Lunch, everybody."

Without thought or hesitation, Stacy turned her head toward the stables and shouted, "Anne, lunch is ready."

"What about me?"

Stacy swiveled around again to stare blankly at him. "What about you?"

"I haven't had lunch, and I'm hungry." Main's voice held a patently false note of wistfulness; his smile oozed boyish charm. "Am I included in Edith's invitation to everybody?"

Stacy felt uncomfortably caught in a cleft stick. On one side, she felt inclined to tell him to go to... the nearest local restaurant, while on the other side, simple good manners demanded she at least give him a meal before summarily ordering him off the property. After all, she reminded herself, the man had come a long way.

"Hello." Main leaned forward to peer with suspiciously bright eyes into her face. "Anyone home?"

"Very funny," Stacy retorted, sourly. But all of her mother's scrupulous instructions on proper behavior rose to haunt her, and Stacy relented, if not exactly graciously. "Oh, all right," she grumbled, walking away from him. "Come along then. You may join us for lunch."

"How could I refuse such a generous invitation?" Main drawled in a dry, mocking tone. "Lead on, dear hostess. I'm right behind you."

And he was... right behind her. Stacy could detect the musky, male scent of him, imagined she could feel the warmth radiating to her from his tightly knit body. An involuntary tremor quaked through her. Damn him, she railed in silent protest. And damn the open shirt exposing his sun-heated broad chest.

* * *

Lunch was a dismal affair, but, fortunately for Stacy's peace of mind, Main remembered to button his shirt before entering the house. Since Anne was moody and withdrawn, the meal would have been a silent one, as well, if not for the seemingly endless supply of questions Edith posed to their guest.

No more forthcoming than Anne, Stacy managed to deflect the occasional remark made to her by replying in monosyllabic grunts. Determined to remain aloof, she tried to block out the sound of their voices, *his* voice, by concentrating on less disturbing matters such as the condition of her favorite horse, the expense of tack and feed for her animals, the vagaries of the spring weather and the contemplation of her navel. But, try as she would, concentrate as she did, odd bits and pieces of the conversation slipped into her awareness.

"This is delicious," Main said at one point, managing to snag Stacy's unwilling attention while complimenting Edith.

"It's only warm-ups." Edith dismissed her efforts with a shrug.

"Warm-ups?" Main turned a baffled look on Stacy.

Reluctant to be drawn into the conversation, but feeling obliged to clarify, Stacy gave him a brief, succinct explanation. "It's leftovers from dinner two nights ago."

"Ah, yes, I see." Main shifted his gaze, and a smile at Edith. "Well, anyway, it is delicious," he repeated. "What's in it, and what do you call it?"

In Stacy's jaundiced opinion, Edith's responsive laugh had more the sound of a girl's simpering giggle.

"It's called Schnitz un Knepp, or Apples and Buttons," the flattered and flushed woman replied. "And it contains ham and pieces of dried apples and small dumplings. It's just plain, stick-to-the-ribs food. Do you really like it?"

"Love it," Main said, proving his claim by holding out his plate for another portion.

Oh, sure, Stacy silently derided, quashing a desire to smirk at him. She knew nothing about him other than that he had come east to Pennsylvania from somewhere in West Texas. Yet there was something about his presence, his obvious self-confidence, an aura of sophistication that convinced Stacy that Jasper Chance was accustomed to finer, more exotic cuisine.

"More coffee, Mr. Chance?"

"Main, please, Edith. And yes, thank you." Now he extended his earthenware coffee mug. "Besides being an excellent cook, you make great coffee."

"Why, thank you . . . Main." Edith twittered, blushing bright pink with pleasure.

Stacy was hard-pressed not to groan aloud. Disdaining the ongoing mutual admiration chatter, she once more attempted to focus her attention elsewhere. It was not to be. Her interest was caught by Edith's very next query.

"Have you made arrangements for the night, Main?"

"Hmm." Main nodded, and continued clearing his plate of every last morsel.

Silence prevailed while he thoroughly chewed his last forkful of food. Then the quiet was shattered by the scraping sound of Anne's chair as she slid it away from the table.

"I'll get back to work," she murmured. "Thanks, Edith. As usual, lunch was very good."

Edith sent a pointed look at the girl's plate. "How would you know?" A frown knit her brows. "You hardly touched it."

"Sorry." Offering the older woman a faint smile, Anne headed for the door.

"Aren't you even going to taste the dessert?" Edith demanded. "It's your favorite."

Anne pulled the screen door open before turning her head to answer. "No, thank you. I...ah...I'm watching my weight."

Edith snorted.

Main stared at the slender young woman in amazement.

Stacy sighed. Obviously the heated words exchanged between Anne and Dan in the stables had upset Anne. The last thing she needed to do was diet— just the opposite, in fact. She had trouble maintaining a healthy weight.

Staring at the now-empty doorway, Stacy decided she would have to talk to her groom, smooth her ruffled sensibilities...as if she didn't have enough on her mind dealing with the Texas interloper.

"I'd like dessert."

Main's request drew Stacy's attention away from her mounting problems, and an immediate reaction from Edith.

"Good," Edith said with approval, jumping out of her chair to bustle to the long countertop. "What about you, Stacy? It's Funeral Pie, made it fresh this morning."

"No, thank you, I..." Stacy's voice faded as she caught the questioning expression on Main's face, saw his lips move as he mouthed the words "Funeral Pie?"

"Raisin pie," she explained.

"Oh." Main's expression switched from questioning to consternation. "I've never heard of raisin pie."

"It's good," Edith said, staunchly.

"Made with raisins," Stacy informed him dryly.

"No doubt," Main said in blanket response. "But why do you call it Funeral Pie?"

"Because it was a staple the women in this area made for gatherings after funerals, since raisins were always available, regardless of the season," Stacy explained.

"Practical," Main said, smiling at Edith as she slid a dessert plate in front of him.

"The Pennsylvania Dutch are practical people," Stacy said, watching his expression change from wary to pleased surprise as he sampled the sweet.

"This is very good." He again complimented Edith before responding to Stacy's assertion. "And what about you? Are you practical, as well?"

"I like to think so." Wondering what, if anything, he was getting at, Stacy warily watched him demolish the generous wedge of pie. But if he had a point to make, it remained unspoken, for Edith stole the initiative from him.

"Talking about practical," she said, "did I understand you to say you have made arrangements for the night?"

"Yes."

Stacy felt a curl of unease unfurl inside her; the man looked altogether too smug and complacent.

"In one of the nearby motels?" Edith persisted.

"No." Main smiled.

The curl of unease flared into alarm inside Stacy.

"Where, then?" Edith asked, voicing the question hammering in Stacy's head.

"I'm staying here."

# Five

―――

"What?" Stacy stared at him in shock.

"I said, I'm staying right here."

"Oh, no, you're not," Stacy stated emphatically, glaring at him.

"Oh, yes, I am," Main retorted.

"But . . . you can't!" Edith protested.

"No?" He arched his brows. "Why not?"

"Because I said no!" Stacy exclaimed.

"Besides, it wouldn't look right, you two alone together in the house." Edith looked scandalized.

Main bypassed Stacy to question the older woman. "You don't live here?"

"No, no," Edith replied, shaking her head. "I have my own home. I live with my husband, up near Lititz. I only come here three days a week."

"Lititz." Main pounced on the place-name. "I'd like to see it. Is it close by?"

"Not too far," Edith answered, distracted from her sense of impropriety by his show of interest. "You turn left at the end of the property road, then right at the inter—"

"Edith!" Stacy interrupted her impatiently. "That's not important right now." She was on her feet and glaring at Main. "You cannot stay here."

"Why can't I? I own a half interest in the place," he reminded her. "If you can stay here, so can I."

Stacy was incensed. "I'm not convinced of the validity of your claim," she said, clenching her teeth against an urgent need to scream in frustration.

"You were not notified?" Main enquired in a maddeningly bland tone.

"Yes, but..."

"Perhaps you should pay a visit to your lawyer," he advised. "Or, better still, give him a call."

"That's exactly what I intend to do." Imposing rigid control on a childish desire to storm from the room, Stacy raised her chin and made a measured, dignified exit.

Nearly an hour later, Stacy stood by the phone, which sat on her cluttered desk, staring into space, attempting to assimilate the surprising information just given to her by her lawyer.

First and foremost of the facts she'd received was, in her attorney's professional opinion, the indisputable legality of Jasper Chance's claim.

Second, but equally surprising, was the information that Jasper was not, in fact, a distant relative, but the grandson of Stacy's grandfather's beloved stepsister.

Stacy shook her head in confusion. She hadn't known her grandfather had a stepsister, had never heard as much as a hint about her.

How could she not have known? Stacy asked herself, baffled by the startling revelation. She had practically grown up on the farm; she and her grandfather had been inseparable. Why had he never mentioned a stepsister? A beloved stepsister?

Deeply hurt by her grandfather's omission, fighting tears, yet trying to understand, Stacy closed her eyes, dredging her mind to recall her attorney's exact words.

"It was all rather mystifying at the beginning," her lawyer, John Knowles had explained. "Which, of course, is the reason I haven't gotten back to you. As a matter of fact, I was planning to contact you this afternoon, since I believe I now have full clarification on the matter."

"But is his claim legal?" Stacy had impatiently asked, despairing the tendency of lawyers to be not only precise but long-winded.

"Oh, yes," he said. "Furthermore, I'm sorry to say, I believe it to be incontestable."

"But how can it be?" Stacy had demanded. "I can't believe my grandfather would ever have added a codicil to his will, leaving half of the farm to a stranger!"

"Yes, well, therein lay the root cause of the mystery presented to me in the letter from Clarence Farraday," he went on ... and on. "You know, the Philadelphia solicitor your grandfather visited?"

"Yes, I know." Somehow, Stacy restrained a loud sigh of exasperation. Add language to the irritating legal, long-winded tendencies, she thought.

"I knew your grandfather for over twenty years, both as friend and legal adviser," Mr. Knowles continued. "And, initially, I also could not conceive of any logical or rational reason for Jacob to suddenly and secretly have a codicil attached to his will, leaving a half portion of the farm to a stranger."

Taking into account the implied and apparent insult to the lawyer's pride and sensibilities, Stacy had managed to refrain from shouting at the man to get on with it. Fortunately he proceeded to do so.

"You must understand, Miss Hunsberger, that the only information I was given when I was initially notified by Mr. Farraday was that he had drawn up the codicil for my client, and the name and location of the bequeathed. Subsequently, while not doubting the veracity of the information, I immediately instigated an investigation into the matter...."

"And?" Stacy had prompted when he paused—either for breath, or effect.

"The results of my investigation were startling, to say the least," Mr. Knowles admitted. "It seems your grandfather did indeed have a stepsister, a young woman ten or so years his senior, whom he adored."

"But, if that is true," Stacy interjected, "why didn't my grandfather ever talk about her, or even mention her name to me?"

"My thoughts exactly, at the time," he replied. "And, from what I could gather, from bits and pieces from old records and the memories of even older residents, as a young woman in her early twenties, she fell in love with an itinerant Texan, who had apparently stopped over in the area on his way back to his home state.''

"A Texan?'' Stacy inserted, shaking her head to dispel a vision of the tall, angular man ensconced in her kitchen, stuffing his face with raisin pie.

"Yes,'' Mr. Knowles confirmed. "And, from all accounts, other than good looks, the man possessed little to recommend him. Your great-grandfather was strongly opposed to a friendship between his stepdaughter and the man, let alone a more intimate relationship. I was informed that he was so furious when the girl ran away with the man, he not only paid a visit to his lawyer to have her name stricken from his will, but also forbade his son from mentioning her name. Since then, no one heard her name from your grandfather's lips. One of the neighbors I spoke with offered the considered opinion that your grandfather was so deeply hurt by his stepsister's action and his father's reaction, that he closed it off, buried it inside, but secretly grieved for his loss of her until the day he died.''

"But that's terrible!'' Stacy cried in protest.

"Yes,'' Mr. Knowles agreed. "But I was told that, not only did your great-grandfather feel betrayed by the girl he had raised as his own child, but that his pride and honor were impugned, as well, since he had already made a tentative agreement with a neighbor for an arranged marriage between the girl and the neighbor's son.''

"How positively Victorian!" Stacy exclaimed, appalled at the very idea.

"Please remember that this all happened over sixty years ago, Miss Hunsberger," the lawyer replied. "Arranged marriages were quite common at the time." He paused, then added, "As a matter of fact, they're not all that uncommon today."

Stacy felt an odd premonitory chill trickle the length of her spine. "You're kidding," she said, while intellectually aware that he wasn't.

"No, I'm not," he said. "It's not unusual for me to draw up several marriage contracts each year."

"But surely not for the old-fashioned, parent-arranged type marriages?"

"In some instances, yes indeed," Mr. Knowles replied—rather pedantically, she thought. "But," he continued, "primarily I'm called upon to draw up more modern arrangements."

"Such as?" Stacy asked, silently assuring herself her interest was merely curiosity.

"Oh, for many and varied reasons," he answered. "There are purely business agreements, in addition to contractual marriages of convenience, for one reason or another...."

His voice went on, but Stacy was no longer listening; her mind was caught, ensnared by the same words Dan had spoken a short time ago—marriage of convenience.

"Miss Hunsberger?" The sharp sound of Mr. Knowles's voice broke into her reverie. "Are you still there?"

"Yes, yes, of course. I'm sorry." Stacy sighed. "I'm a little scattered at the moment."

"Understandable, under the circumstances," he replied in tones of commiseration.

"What you're telling me is that you believe I haven't got an ice cube's chance in hell of contesting the will," she said, stifling another sigh. "Right?"

"Well, I wouldn't use that exact phrasing," he said. "But in my considered opinion, yes."

And there it was, the pronouncement that shattered Stacy's hopes of claiming sole ownership of the property, and dislodging her unwelcome houseguest.

The conversation with Mr. Knowles had proved informative, enlightening and depressing. Tears slid down Stacy's cheeks, unnoticed and unchecked—tears of sympathy for her grandfather, and also tears for herself and the uncomfortable situation she now found herself in. Like it or not, it appeared she was stuck with the Texan.

And Stacy didn't like it. Not one damn bit.

Main sat sprawled at the kitchen table, nursing his third cup of coffee. Edith had left the room after refilling his cup, declaring she had work to do. Over an hour had elapsed since Stacy swept from the room, looking for all the world like a queen displeased by a member of her court.

And he had displeased her with his stated intention of staying at the farm.

Main felt the stab of his conscience, and he shifted uncomfortably on the hardwood chair. What had he expected, to be welcomed with open arms? an inner voice demanded. He had figured that she'd resent him. He was a stranger, and a usurper into the bargain. How would he have felt, if the circumstances were reversed?

Mad, Main acknowledged honestly. Damned mad. In fairness, Main conceded that, in her place, he would be raising all kinds of hell with his lawyer.

Which was, he suspected, precisely what Stacy was doing at that very moment.

Main couldn't, and didn't blame Stacy for fighting for what she believed was rightfully hers. He'd have done the same in her position.

By all that was right and just, Main knew he should reject the inheritance, sign his half interest over to Stacy—all neat and legal—and go back to Texas.

A wry smile slanted across his lips. In point of fact, disclaiming his rights to the surprising inheritance sight unseen had been his original intent. Main had even consulted a lawyer about doing just that.

But Main had changed his mind at the last minute before signing the document of release. The laid-back ambience of West Texas had begun to pall. The old restlessness had taken hold of him, that inner command urging him to move, get on with his interrupted search for that special somewhere.

Never would Main have dreamed that he'd find his somewhere on a horse farm in Pennsylvania. Yet, here it was. He had recognized it at once. Here was home.

Main not only understood Stacy's anger and resentment, he sympathized, empathized with her. But now, after seeing the place, breathing the place, feeling the place all the way to the marrow of his bones, he could not give it up.

Main was home, and he was determined to stay.

He and Stacy would have to work something out, Main decided. Together, they would have to come up with some kind of workable arrangement. What that arrangement would be, he had no idea. Possibly something would come to light as they discussed the problem.

If they ever got around to discussing the problem, he thought grumpily.

Main shot an impatient look at the old-fashioned schoolroom clock on the kitchen wall.

What the hell was keeping her?

Ten minutes later, Main was pushing his chair away from the table, prepared to search the house for her, when Stacy walked into the room, her demeanor the complete opposite of her earlier sweeping queenly exit.

But what struck Main, causing a sharper jab in his conscience, was the defeated, haunted look of her. Her eyes were suspiciously bright and her pale cheeks retained the evidence of tear tracks. Her soft mouth curved in a sad angle. Her shoulders were squared, too tightly, as though held erect by sheer willpower. Without a word being spoken he knew, and yet he asked the obvious.

"So what did your lawyer have to say?"

Stacy flinched as if struck, but she met his gaze with direct honesty.

"He said your claim is legal and, in his professional opinion, incontestable."

Her voice was low but rock steady, earning Main's admiration, and sorely testing his determination. He ached for Stacy with a feeling of deep compassion unlike anything he had ever before experienced. He felt an urge to draw her into his arms, into his protection, to comfort her, reassure her, promise her anything, everything, if only to put the sparkle back in her eyes. For a fleeting instant, he was even tempted to hand his inheritance over to her.

Fortunately for Main, Stacy chose that same instant to elaborate on her conversation with her lawyer.

"He also explained the circumstances, and the relationship between your grandmother and my grandfather." Stacy swallowed with visible difficulty before adding, "I . . . I'm sorry. I honestly didn't know."

Main was suddenly alert, and full of terse, hardedged questions. "Circumstances? What circumstances?" Threads of bewilderment were woven through his tight voice. "And what exactly do you mean in regards to a relationship between my grandmother and your grandfather?"

Stacy's eyes grew wide with startled surprise. "You didn't know, either?"

"What are you implying?" Main's eyelids narrowed over eyes glittering with suspicion and anger. "If you are suggesting something illicit . . . immoral—"

"No! No!" Stacy interrupted him in sharp denial. "It was nothing at all like that. There was no blood tie, or physical attraction. He was still a boy at the time, and she was already a young woman."

"Then how was it?" Main's voice still held a hard, steely edge. "Explain it to me."

Stacy drew a deep breath, and then briefly and concisely repeated the information her lawyer had imparted to her. When she was finished, she sighed and shrugged. "I honestly didn't know. My grandfather never mentioned her name to me."

"And my grandmother never mentioned his name to me, or even that she had at one time lived in Pennsylvania," Main said, unconsciously echoing her sigh. "Until my lawyer told me that she had been born here, I had always believed she was a native of Tyler, Texas."

"Tyler?" Stacy frowned. "I thought Tyler was somewhere in North Texas."

"It is."

Her eyes revealed her confusion. "But I was told you were from West Texas."

"I was born in Tyler, but I'd been living in West Texas since last fall," Main explained. "I suppose that's why it took so long for Mr. Farraday's letter to catch up to me." His smile was wry. "It first went to Tyler, then New York City and finally to West Texas."

Stacy's eyes grew bright with the light of expectation. "You move around a lot?"

"I used to," Main admitted, ruthlessly tamping down another nudge from his conscience. "But don't get your hopes up, sweetheart," he went on, flat-voiced, swearing in frustrated silence as he watched the light fade from her expressive eyes. "I like what I see here, and I have no plans of moving on in the near future, maybe not ever."

"Not even if I offer to buy you out?" Stacy asked, knowing full well she lacked the resources to do so.

Recalling the fence posts that needed to be replaced and the few other signs of disrepair he'd noticed, Main arched one brow skeptically and responded to her question with one of his own. "You have the where-withal to make such an offer?"

Caught in the trap of her own making, Stacy lowered her eyes and stared at the scuffed toes of her boots. Admitting to Dan that she was broke had been embarrassing; admitting it to this man was flat-out humiliating. She contemplated lying to him, while raking her mind for a way, other than mortgaging the farm and the animals left on it, to raise the considerable amount of cash necessary to back up her offer, but innate honesty forced her to answer truthfully.

"No."

"That's what I figured." A gentle smile softened his hard lip line. "You're pretty much working on a shoe-string here," he probed. "Aren't you?"

Stacy's head snapped up. Pride blazed from her eyes, changing the soft hazel color to a gemstone green. "Yes, I am," she admitted defiantly. "But I can—"

"You need working capital." He cut her off with hard practicality, fighting the sudden urge to draw her into his arms, this time for an altogether different, purely physical, reason. The sight of her, eyes blazing with defiance, pride stiffening her spine, tormented his suddenly responsive senses and tested his control.

In that instant, on the spot in that kitchen, Main wanted Stacy—all of her. And it was damned surprising, considering how long it had been since he'd wanted any woman. His arms ached to hold her softness against his hard, tight body. His mouth tingled with a need to taste her pouting, rebellious lips. His body throbbed with hot desire to be a part of hers.

Surprising indeed. And Stacy wasn't even close to the description of his preferred type!

Main drew a slow, hopefully calming breath. "You need a ready cash flow."

"Yes." The evident strain of her voice revealed how very close she was to the end of her tether.

"You have no supplemental income source?"

"Supplemental source?" she repeated, frowning. "I don't understand. Like what?"

Main smiled. "Securities, employment."

"No," Stacy said, shrugging. "My grandfather didn't invest. I was employed, of course, but I gave up my job a few months ago to concentrate on getting the farm back in order."

"And now the money you did have is gone?"

"Yes."

"I have it."

Stacy blinked. "Have it?" she repeated, uncertain if he meant the cash or a solution. "Have what?"

"The working capital." Main's smile was chiding. "The wherewithal. Ready funds. Cash. *M-o-n-e-y.*" He spelled the last word out.

"But—" Stacy broke off as she drew herself up, shoulders squared, spine rigid, chin raised and tilted at a proud angle. "I can't accept..."

"I'm not suggesting a loan." He again interrupted her, his voice rough with need cloaked in impatience.

Stacy narrowed her eyes with suspicion. "Then, what exactly are you suggesting?"

# Six

Main couldn't resist an urge to laugh; she looked so...so damned nervous and wary. But, in truth, he wasn't sure himself exactly what he was suggesting. He was groping in the dark, blindly following instinctive directives. His careless-looking shrug conveyed more of his uncertain feeling than Stacy could have possibly known.

"Nothing illegal or immoral," he drawled, stalling for time to come up with a plausible plan.

"I'm relieved to hear it." Though Stacy's tone was dry and sarcastic, the truth of her words was evident in the easing of tension in her tight expression and taut body. She waited, a second, and then another. When he was not forthcoming with an explanation, she broke and snapped, "I'm waiting for an answer, Mr. Chance. What do you have in mind?"

There was a glimmering of an idea teasing the outer rim of Main's consciousness; it was undefined, not fully formed, and yet, so startling, he wasn't even sure he cared to draw it out or probe the breadth and depth of it.

But Stacy was waiting, impatiently if the staccato tap-tapping of her booted right toe was any indication to go by. Then her eyes narrowed, the tapping suddenly ceased and she burst out in a small explosion.

"Well? Spit it out, Texan!"

Main frowned, feeling pressured. Damn! She was one pushy dame, he thought, skirting around the edges of the idea that, on mere cursory examination, he couldn't quite believe his mind had conceived.

"Ah . . . yes, well . . ." He procrastinated, amazed at the scope and future difficulties inherent in the emerging concept. "I was thinking that . . . perhaps, it would be to our—"

"Stacy, could you come down to the stables?"

Saved by the groom! Expelling a chest-constricting breath, Main swung in unison with Stacy to stare at the anxious-faced young woman.

"What is it, Anne?" Stacy was moving toward the girl before the screen door banged shut behind her. "What's wrong?"

"It's Hammerhead," Anne said, gulping a quick breath. "He's stepping funny with his right hind leg."

"Hammerhead?" Main was beside Stacy with two long strides, following at her heels as she rushed from the house.

"The stallion," Stacy said distractedly, taking off at a trot along the footpath that cut through the side yard, halving the distance of the graveled road to the stables.

Hammerhead? Main came to a dead stop. Hammerhead! His laughter started as a low rumble in his chest then burst forth in a roar of delight.

"Hammerhead," he repeated, catching up to Stacy near the stables.

She tossed him a dry look. "Yes, Hammerhead, with all its obvious connotations," she confirmed, in an equally dry tone of voice. "On occasion, my grandfather displayed a wry and blatantly wicked sense of humor."

"I'm sorry I never met him," Main said, dogging her footsteps to a corral adjacent to the stables. "He must have been an interesting character."

"He was," Stacy said, coming to a stop at the corral fence. "He was both interesting and autocratic," she went on, staring intently at the single animal inside the enclosed area.

Coming to a halt beside her at the railed fence, Main ran an encompassing look over the huge stallion. He was a handsome beast. His muscles rippled beneath the rich brown coat gleaming in the bright afternoon sunlight. His sleek neck was arched, his large head cocked, his eyes rolled, casting a wary look at his human spectators. And then he moved to dance away and there was a noticeable favoring of his right hind leg.

"Maybe he picked up a stone," Main observed, his sharp gaze catching the careful way the animal placed his right rear hoof on the ground.

"Looks like it," Stacy said, letting him know she also hadn't missed the horse's gingerly step. She turned to the girl standing on the other side of her at the fence. "Did you check his hoof for a stone?"

Anne shook her head. "I'm not going in there with him," she said, backing away from the fence.

Stacy made a short, impatient move with one hand. "I've told you before that there's nothing to be afraid of, Anne. You know he won't hurt you."

"No," Anne said, shaking her head in denial. "I know he won't hurt *you.*"

A faint smile of understanding tilting her lips, Stacy placed a hand on the top rail. "Okay, I'll look," she said, stepping onto the bottom rail.

"No, I'll look," Main said, vaulting lithely over the fence and landing lightly on the balls of his feet before she had swung one leg over the top rail.

"Be careful!" Stacy cried. "He could be dangerous to someone he doesn't know."

Main wasn't listening. He was sauntering toward the animal, crooning in a low, soothing tone. "You are one magnificent piece of horseflesh, fella, even if you do have a dumb name," he chanted, holding out his hand, palm up, as he approached the quivering horse. "But you're hurting now, and I want to help. Will you let me?"

The animal nuzzled Main's palm with utter delicacy, then he blew a loud, moist snort and cast Main a baleful look when he found no treat there.

Main chuckled. "Next time, big guy, and that's a promise," he murmured, gliding his palm up the animal's head, then down his arched neck. "Is it a deal?" he went on, still in a soft, beguiling tone. Taking infinite patience, and long, gentle strokes, Main worked his way to the animal's hind quarters. He squatted as he carefully examined the leg in question, and grunted with satisfaction when he found no apparent signs of strain or injury.

"Okay, let's have a look," Main said softly, when at last he was able to raise Hammerhead's hoof for inspection. "Ah-hah," he exclaimed in a near whisper on his discovery of a small, sharp-edged stone lodged beneath the hoof. "Be a good, dumb-named horse now," he sang, plucking the stone free with long, slim but strong fingers. Then, "There you go," he said, lowering the hoof to the ground. "I don't see a break or bruise in the flesh."

Swinging his head around, the horse gave Main a nudge, as if to say thanks, then shook out his flowing dark mane and pranced away. Laughing to himself, Main strolled back to the two women waiting for him at the fence.

Stacy's breathing returned to normal as Main loped toward her. She had at first feared that his action was motivated by masculine bravado when he'd leapt the fence, but it had soon become obvious that he possessed more than a smattering of experience with horses.

Even so, Stacy had stood, immobile and barely breathing the entire time he'd worked with the animal, for though she knew Hammerhead was not usually a fractious animal, one could never be certain of any horse, especially a powerful, high-mettled stallion.

Even though her breath came more effortlessly, Stacy felt her heartbeat flutter as she watched Main approach in that easy, loose-limbed gait. The sight of him caused a sheen of perspiration on her palms and forehead, and a hollow sensation in her midsection. The rippling movement of the muscles in his thighs drew her reluctant but appreciative gaze to the lower portion of his body, from his narrow waist and flat, almost concave belly and slim hips to his long legs.

*There was a powerhouse of raw sensuality packed into his lower anatomy.*

Shocked by the errant thought, and growing warmer by the second, Stacy dragged her gaze up the length of his body, skimming over the breadth of his flat, muscled chest and his broad shoulders, and coming to a breath-catching halt on the chiseled outline of his masculine mouth.

*What would it be like, feeling her soft lips crushed beneath that hard male mouth?*

The speculative thought sent a hot streak of awareness from the base of her spine to the back of her head.

What in the world was the matter with her? Stacy demanded of herself, trying to ignore the tingling anticipatory sensation dancing over her scalp. She had never ever felt anything in particular at the sight of a man's—any man's—mouth . . . or any other part of a male body, for that matter.

Shaken by her unusual physical and sensory response, Stacy pushed the erratic thoughts aside, carefully composing herself as he drew near to the fence.

"It was a stone," Main said, again vaulting effortlessly over the top rail. "No damage done."

"Personally, I wouldn't trust that stallion any farther than I could throw him," Anne said, flashing a

grin at Main. "You either know your way around
horses, mister, or you've got more guts than brains."

"Anne!" Stacy admonished, in an obviously token
chastisement, that left little doubt that she agreed with
the younger woman's assessment.

Still grinning, Anne pushed away from the fence and
headed toward the stables. "I calls 'em as I sees 'em,"
she shot back before disappearing inside the building.

Main was lazily propped against the fence, laughing
softly at Anne's gibe. He cocked a questioning brow at
Stacy when she turned to give him a look that was every
bit as baleful as Hammerhead's had been.

"Don't encourage her," she said, swinging away
from the fence to return to the house.

"No? Why not?" Main drawled, gliding an appreciative glance over her sweetly curved undulating bottom before falling into step beside her.

"She's already fresh enough," she retorted. "She
drives Dan to distraction."

"I noticed."

"And I couldn't help but notice how well you han-
dled yourself in the corral," she retorted. "You do
know your way around horses, don't you?"

"Some," Main admitted. "I ran a rental stable for
a spell in West Texas."

Stacy slid a frowning glance at him as she mounted
the steps and crossed the porch. "I thought that maybe
you had grown up on a ranch."

"I'd be willing to bet that most easterners believe
that every Texan lives on a ranch." Main's grin was as
wicked as her grandfather's sense of humor, and as

devastating. "I grew up in town, wore shoes and everything."

"Okay, point made and taken," she conceded, pulling open the door and ushering him in with a sweeping move of her free arm. "I stand corrected."

"Enlightened," he drawled, still grinning.

"Right." Stacy gave a quick nod of her head. "Now perhaps you'd be so kind as to enlighten me about what you had in mind with your earlier suggestion."

Damn. The grin vanished from Main's face. Stacy had neatly cornered him. He knew it. She knew it. He knew she knew it. She knew he knew it. And he knew she knew he knew it.

Helluva state, Main mused, shuffling through his thoughts for clarification. He didn't need to shuffle too strenuously. Hell, he didn't even have to cut the mental deck, so to speak. His glimmer of an idea had blossomed into full light while he'd been tending to the stallion.

The resumed tap-tapping of Stacy's toe caught Main's attention, telling him his hedging time had run out. Still, he made another bid for a few minutes more—time in which to get his thoughts in order.

"Look, could I wash up before we talk?" he said, raising his dirt-caked hands.

Stacy's eyes flickered and she looked startled, as though only then becoming aware that they were standing just inside the kitchen door.

"Yes, yes, of course." Her wan smile held self-derision. "You can wash up in here," she said, turning to walk to the double-sink.

What did he have in mind? The question nagged at Stacy as she stood at the sink beside him. He was too close, much too close. She couldn't think—think?—she could barely breathe!

Stacy didn't like the feelings and sensations his nearness created inside her. Nor did she appreciate the impact on her senses from the earthy scent of him, the too-attractive look of him, or the sheer overpowering masculine sexuality he exuded by merely standing there, scrubbing his hands.

Jasper Chance had a strange heady effect on her unlike anything Stacy had ever before experienced with a man. Even in the mundane act of washing their hands, there was a sense of intimacy surrounding them that unnerved her.

What was it about this particular man? Stacy asked herself, edging away from him as she dried her hands. An unwarranted tingle crept up her spine when he followed her to the trash can; the tingle shot down her arms and into her fingers when the back of his hand brushed hers as he dropped the paper towel into the can.

Again, he was too close. The warmth of his body enveloped her. Stacy stepped aside, swallowing against a sudden tightness in her throat.

"Your...er, suggestion?" she prompted, despairing the break in her voice, the breathless sound of it.

His smile was gentle, yet had the power of a body blow in it. Stacy felt the reverberating effects all the way to the soles of her boots.

"This might take a while," he said, slanting a glance at the table. "Could we sit down...have some coffee?"

"Yes, yes, of course," Stacy said, glad to have something to do, and a reason for moving away from him. "Have a seat. I'll make the coffee."

Stacy was suddenly all thumbs. She, the woman who had always been praised by everyone for her swift and sure efficiency, was all at once seemingly incapable of retrieving two cups from the wall cabinet without rattling them together, or filling the automatic coffeemaker's glass pot without banging it against the cold-water faucet.

What was it about this man? Stacy repeated to herself, scowling as she fumbled with the basket liners. So, okay, he possessed a certain rugged attractiveness. But she knew many attractive men. Dan Slater was one of them. Yet she had never become all quivery and inept while around any one of them, including Dan.

So, if it wasn't his looks, what then was it about Jasper Chance that unnerved and rattled her? Stacy pondered, absently raising the pot to pour the water into the grate on top of the coffeemaker.

*He's sexy as hell.*

The thought seared through Stacy's mind, causing a tremor throughout her entire body, which, in turn, caused her to splash some of the water over the lip of the grate.

"Wouldn't that taste better if you'd put some coffee grounds into the basket?"

"Huh?" Blinking, Stacy lowered her gaze to the pot, which was slowly filling with clear water. "Oh, hell," she muttered, calling herself the world's biggest dip-stick.

"Would you like some help?" Main's voice was measured, polite and loaded with silent laughter. "I've been told that I make terrific coffee."

*Have you been told that you make terrific love, as well?*

Stacy clamped her lips together to keep from groaning aloud. What was it with her and these erotic speculations all of a sudden? she asked herself, staring at the pot in helpless wonder. Was she cracking under the recent strain or—

"Stacy?"

Main's soft call snagged her fractured attention. There was no help for it; she would have to face him sooner or later. Swallowing to moisten her parched throat, Stacy drew a steadying breath and slowly turned around.

"I asked if you'd like some help?" Main's voice was soft, but his eyes were sharp, glittering gray lasers piercing into her eyes, as if to see into her mind.

What little there was left of her mind, Stacy told herself. Rescue in the form of humor rushed in to save her from making an absolute idiot of herself. She slid a glance to the pot of hot water, then back to him.

"Are you sure you wouldn't like a bracing cup of fresh hot water?" She grinned at him, and was gratified to feel the tension drain from her. "I've been told it's good for the digestive tract . . . or something."

"Mmm-hmm," Main murmured, returning her grin.

Stacy laughed outright. "Not buying that, huh?"

"Nope," he confessed, laughing with her.

"O-kay," she said, pulling a long face. "I guess I'll just have to start over."

"Can I help?" Main was sliding his chair away from the table as he asked.

"No!" Stacy gave a quick shake of her head. "I'm nothing if not determined," she said, meaning, of course, that she was determined to hang on to her equilibrium by keeping him at a reasonable distance. "Er... I see there's some pie left," she said to distract him. "Help yourself."

Main followed the direction of her gaze to the covered pie plate on the countertop. His grin became wolfish. "You talked me into it."

By blocking him out of her mind, and concentrating for all she was worth, Stacy finally managed to produce the coffee. Fortunately, it not only smelled wonderful, but tasted as good as it smelled.

"Hmm, delicious," Main pronounced after taking a tentative sip of the steaming brew. "And worth the wait."

"Thank you." Seated opposite him, Stacy sipped at her own cup of coffee, while she waited for him to finish eating the generous wedge of pie he'd cut for himself. Anxiety was building inside her about the "suggestion" he had, concerning their situation.

"I could become addicted to that," Main admitted, grinning at her as he pushed his plate aside and reached for his coffee. "I have a sweet tooth, you know."

"I'd have never guessed," Stacy drawled, recalling the two large slices he'd devoured mere hours ago. "Are you ready to explain your suggestion now?"

Her anxious feeling expanded as the grin faded from his face, replaced by a contemplative expression. Instinct warned her that she wasn't going to like whatever it was he had in mind.

"We need to have a serious discussion about this."

"About what?" she snapped, close now to the limits of her patience.

Main gave her a chiding look. "Why, about our situation, of course. I was dead serious earlier when I told you I intended to stay here."

Stacy bristled, but kept a rein on her temper by reminding herself that he was, in fact, co-owner of the place. Her sigh had the sound of defeat. "All right, I'll ask Edith if she can stay over tonight."

"Tonight?" Main's arched brows shot up. "I didn't mean I was only planning on staying the night. I have no intentions of being an absentee partner."

Stacy's stomach clenched; so did her teeth. Prying them apart she asked, "What are your intentions?"

He looked surprised, as though the answer were or should be obvious.

"Why, I intend to stay here...permanently."

# Seven

———

"**P**ermanently!"

Stacy sat listening to the shocked sound of her own voice echoing inside her head, while staring at him in slack-jawed astonishment.

"Yes, permanently," Main reiterated.

"But... but..." Stacy paused to swallow, and consider her precarious position. Had she really believed he would stay at the farm one night, then return to Texas? Yes, she conceded, even though the belief hadn't been fully formed in her mind. Although he had mentioned managing a stable in West Texas, Jasper Chance just didn't look the type to interest himself with the day-to-day operation of running a small horse farm. To Stacy, he had more the look of the big city and fast action.

"That's why I said we need to have a serious discussion," Main said, breaking her introspection.

"You also said you had a suggestion to make," she reminded him in a testy tone. "Something to do with working capital, cash, the wherewithal?"

"I do."

Stacy felt milliseconds away from tearing out her hair...or his. "Were you planning on telling me about it anytime soon?" She shot a glance at the wall clock. "The day's wearing on," she groused, her expression clearly conveying that he was wearing on her nerves, as well.

"My suggestion concerns what I believe could be a viable working arrangement, but first..." Main hesitated, mentally sifting through the possible, and even probable ramifications of his original idea—to incorporate their co-ownership of the property into a full partnership by means of a contractual marriage arrangement...startling and wild as the idea still was to him. Where had the idea sprung from? He barely knew her. But then, what difference did it make? He wasn't looking for a love match; he was looking for a home. But he had just been given that, by inheritance. He didn't need to offer marriage to acquire it. And yet...why not?

For his part, and in light of his ambiguous feelings concerning the concept of romantic love, Main considered his idea to be the most logical and workable solution. Marriage to Stacy would put the stamp of permanence and belonging on his ownership. And he felt positive they could make it work. But Main had enough experience with women to realize that the female of the species had a tendency to regard marriage from an emotional rather than a practical point of view.

In addition, Main acknowledged the very real fact of the briefness of their acquaintance. Other than the information Stacy had received from her lawyer, she knew nothing about him. By the same token, he knew virtually nothing about her. He had wondered if she had something going with Dan; for all Main knew, she could be seriously involved, engaged or even . . .

"Arrangement?" Stacy prompted, breaking into his introspection to end the lengthy silence. "What kind of an arrangement do you have in mind?"

"I'll explain shortly," he began, hedging for time to pull his speculative meanderings into some sort of cohesive conclusions. Fortunately, for him, Edith chose that moment to bustle into the kitchen.

"Oh, you're here, Stacy," the older woman said, sparing a smile for Main. "I was just coming to find you, to tell you that I'm leaving now."

"Now?" Stacy glanced at the clock. "But it's only three-thirty and . . ."

"And I asked you on Monday if you'd mind if I left at three-thirty on Friday," Edith inserted. "Remember?"

Stacy grimaced. "I do now," she admitted. "But, until you reminded me, I forgot today is Friday."

"You've had a lot on your mind," Edith said, slanting a sly, sidelong glance at Main.

"Hmm, ah, yes," Stacy murmured, choking back laughter at the naturally straightforward woman's inept attempt at subtlety, and Main's obvious amusement in response to it. "You and George are meeting friends for dinner, aren't you?"

"That's right." Edith fairly beamed. "We haven't seen Bev and Donald since they retired to Florida two years ago." She glanced at the clock. "And I'd better get a move on. I want to stop at the State store for a bottle of wine," she said, heading for the door. "I'll see you Monday." She hesitated, holding the door open, arching her gray eyebrows as she looked at Main. "Will I be seeing you, too?"

"I wouldn't be a bit surprised," he drawled. "Have a good time this evening."

"Yes, have fun," Stacy concurred, managing a smile for the woman even though she suddenly felt more than a little apprehensive about her own evening.

"Why, thank you, Mr.—Main," Edith said, flushing. "And you, too, Stacy." She stepped onto the porch, then paused once more to call back, "Oh! I almost forgot! Your supper's in the fridge. All you have to do is nuke it."

Main turned to Stacy with a puzzled look as the screen door slammed shut. "Nuke it?"

"Shove it into the microwave oven," she explained absently, raking her mind for a polite way of telling him that under the circumstances he couldn't stay the night. Stacy might as well have saved herself the effort for, anticipating her reaction to the situation, he beat her to the draw.

"I'm staying." His voice was flat, hard, unrelenting. "With or without a chaperon."

Stacy couldn't deny his right to stay. It hurt, more than she'd have believed possible, to admit that by her grandfather's legal decree, Main was entitled to half of everything, in the house and on the property. Resentment came to a boil inside her, and she didn't even try to conceal it.

"And you couldn't care less that my reputation won't be worth spit, do you?" She demanded.

Main gave her a wry look. "Get real, Stacy," he taunted. "You know as well as I do that it's no big deal today for a man and a woman to live together. It's common practice."

"Not for me it isn't!" she retorted. "I dread the thought of what people will think or say."

"Why the hell should you care what people think or say?" Main shot back at her.

"Because I live here, grew up here with these people," she cried. "This is my home!"

"And now it's going to be my home, too," he reminded her. "But be assured that I won't allow anyone to dictate to me how I'm to live."

Stacy was beaten, she knew she was beaten, and still she fought on. "You could at least do the decent thing and stay in a motel until I can make other arrangements."

Main arched one skeptical brow. "You can afford to hire a full-time sleep-in housekeeper?"

"No," Stacy reluctantly confessed, glaring at him in hot resentment.

"Okay, I'll spring for a housekeeper," Main offered with casual generosity. But before she could digest his offer, he softly added, "You fire Edith."

The taste of utter defeat was terrible, but Stacy had little choice than to swallow it. "I can't do that. Edith first came to work here for my grandfather over twenty years ago. I can't remember a time when she wasn't here.''

At least Main had the grace not to crow. "So that puts us right back on square one, doesn't it?"

"All right!" Stacy exploded, breaking under the pressure. "You have the legal right to do whatever you want to do. I can't stop you. Stay the night. Stay forever," she cried, hating the broken sound of her voice. "I'll move out!"

"Dammit, Stacy. Stop talking like a fool!" Main barked. "There's no reason for you to move out. I told you before that I have a suggestion on how to resolve this." Main hesitated, certain that now was hardly the time to mention his original idea. "I just need some time to think."

"What's to think about?" she retorted. "This farm has belonged to Hunsbergers for over two hundred years. I spent nearly half my life here with my grandfather. The land, this house were a second home to me." Stacy blinked against the sudden hot sting of tears. "Now it's my only home."

"I'm sorry." Though Main's expression of sympathy was sincere, his determination to take up residence on the property remained adamant.

"No you're not." Stacy could hear the sound of petulance in her voice, but she was past caring. "If you were really sorry, you'd leave here and be satisfied with taking your share of whatever profit the farm shows each month."

"Profit?" Main's tone and expression conveyed blatant disbelief. "Your books show a profit?"

Stacy lowered her eyes to avoid his knowing stare. "Well, not for the past couple months," she admitted, grudgingly. "But I've had so much to do since Gramps died, so much paperwork." She raised accusing eyes to his. "And then there was all the confusion about your claim, I—"

"How many stallions besides Hammerhead do you have?" Main interrupted her to ask.

Stacy's eyelids flickered, but she maintained his laser sharp gaze. "None."

"One stallion," he murmured, shaking his head. "And how many mares?"

"Five," she replied in a whisper.

"Five mares and one stallion." Main heaved a tired-sounding sigh. "And you seriously expect to show a profit?"

Stacy bristled. "No, of course not. Regardless of what you may think, I'm not a fool."

"I didn't think you were." Main shrugged. "But...I suspect that you might have entertained the hope that I was...if not a fool, then ignorant of the horse business."

Stacy didn't refute his assessment for, while she hadn't given a lot of thought to his possible experience, she had unthinkingly assumed it to be minimal.

"I find it hard to believe that your grandfather survived all these years with such a limited operation," Main observed when she didn't respond.

"He didn't," Stacy muttered. "I mean, my grandfather didn't have a limited operation," she explained. "He always kept at least two, but normally three, stallions and never less than ten or twelve mares."

Main frowned, and voiced an assumption. "You've been forced to sell off stock to clear some debts?"

Stacy resented his questioning, even while she acknowledged his right to the information. Her resentment was evident, in her closed expression and in the tightness of her tone. "No. My grandfather slowly sold off the stock during the last six months of his life."

"Was he in debt?"

"My grandfather?" Stacy exclaimed. "Never! He adhered to the old principle of paying cash or doing without."

"Then why sell over half of his stock?" Main demanded with growing impatience and puzzlement. "You're not making much sense, you know."

"I'm not certain, but..." Stacy paused. She felt pressured, cornered and sensed an overriding need to move. Pushing her chair away from the table, she stood and walked to the screen door, to stare out at the view she loved, and inward at bittersweet memories and images of the tough but loving, autocratic but indulgent grandfather she'd adored.

*Why did you have to die, Gramps?*

"But...what?"

The man her grandfather had selected, for whatever reason, to share her inheritance, intruded into her swirling memories with his persistence.

Stacy blinked back a fresh surge of tears. She'd be damned before she'd tell Main about the theory Dan had come up with, which she had subsequently accepted as probable. Instead, she decided to give him the reason she had at first believed to be her grandfather's motive.

"I think he sold the stock for my benefit," she finally answered, damning the break in her voice.

"You've lost me, sweetheart." Main's chair made a scraping noise on the tiled floor. "How could selling the stock possibly benefit you?"

"Don't call me sweetheart." She automatically protested his meaningless endearment.

"Answer my question," he retorted softly, ignoring her objection.

She heard him, felt him cross the floor to her. A tremor rippled through her body. "My grandfather knew that I was barely making ends meet on the salary I earned in my position of assistant to the manager of a famous designer outlet store in Reading, never mind any savings to talk about. And I believe he wanted to have the cash available for me, because he knew I would need it." Stacy closed her eyes as the warm tears spilled over and ran down her cheeks.

"Were you in debt over your head?"

Damning his persistence, her own weakness and her scalding tears, Stacy stiffened her spine against the recurring shiver and muttered, "No."

"Then ... why?" he insisted.

Let me alone! she cried in silent agony.

"Stacy?"

The scalding tears came faster. Stacy broke, her voice revealing the pain of loss. "I ... I believe that my gramps knew he was going to die. He didn't believe in the concept of life insurance, said they were gambling that a person would live a long time, while said person was betting he wouldn't. He knew I'd need the money for taxes, legal fees and..." She swallowed; it hurt. "And for his funeral."

"Are you crying?"

He was close, too close. Stacy could feel his warm breath ruffle her hair, could smell the distinct male scent of him. She shook her head in silent denial and bit down hard on her lip, but the flow of tears streamed unabated.

"Ah, hell, Stacy," Main muttered, grasping her shoulder to turn her around to face him. "Don't cry." He stared down at her wet cheeks for a heart-stopping moment, then, heaving a sigh, he drew her into his arms. "I didn't come here to deliberately hurt you. We'll work something out."

Stacy hadn't expected compassion or warmth or comfort from him. His show of all three expressions was her ultimate undoing. All the grief of losing her beloved grandfather, which she had thus far managed to hold at bay, and all the pain she'd suffered on learning about the codicil he had added to his will, combined to overwhelm her. Giving way to the wracking sobs, Stacy cried all over the front of Main's soft shirt.

Main didn't mind. In fact, he was barely aware of the dampness of his shirt, simply because he was much too aware of the enticing softness of her body pressing against him, as if seeking shelter from a storm. A pang of what—sympathy? No, a much stronger emotion shot through him when she tried to speak between choking gasps.

"I . . . I'm . . . sorry." Her words were muffled by his shirt. "Sometimes I'll hear a noise and I'll look around, expecting to see him standing there, smiling at me, loving me, and I can't stand the thought that I'll never see him smile at me again. The house is so empty without him...so lonely. He was all I had and I...I miss him so much . . . so very . . ." Her voice was lost in the sodden material.

A feeling of protectiveness unlike anything Main had ever experienced rose inside him. Tightening his left arm to draw her closer to him, he stroked Stacy's hair, her shoulders, her back, and murmured reassurances to her.

"Shh, it's all right," he crooned. "Cry it all out. The house won't be empty anymore. I'm here. I'll help. You'll see. Everything will be all right."

Lord! Main thought, no longer aware of what he was saying. She was so soft, so pliant, and he was so hard—the muscles in his shoulders, arms, stomach and thighs were bunched and taut, so hard, so...

Damn! His body was responding in the most obvious, blatant way to the pressure of her soft curves against his stronger, muscular, more angular frame. Why had his libido picked this inopportune moment to kick with such demanding force back into active duty?

It wasn't fair to her, Main thought in self-disgust, exerting every ounce of willpower to control the quickening of his body. Stacy was seeking shelter, not sensuality, within the haven of his embrace, trusting him with what he suspected was her first surrender to her shattering grief over the loss of her beloved grandfather.

Knowing she couldn't miss the evidence of his arousal, Main expected Stacy to step back. Instead, she snuggled even closer, igniting a fire in his body that raced out of control throughout his bloodstream to converge in a molten pool in his loins.

Main had endured a long dry spell without physical release. He had been emotionally and physically drained when he'd left New York. Subsequently, he had drifted through the fall, winter and early spring months feeling nothing but the most negligible interest in any one female—which he had not acted upon. He had remained celibate by choice.

Now, from all indications, Main's days of celibacy were swiftly nearing an end. He wanted Stacy with a bone-deep intensity unlike anything he had ever before felt. Shaken by that very intensity, Main gritted his teeth, and fought a silent battle with his natural instincts.

Stacy, on the other hand, was blissfully, if momentarily, unaware of the inner war being waged by her unexpected comforter. For the first time in months, she felt safe, protected from the buffeting winds of nearly unbearable sorrow and subsequent crushing circumstances.

Not even with Dan had she been able to let go of the searing sense of loss and the specter of fear of failure haunting her every waking and sleeping moment.

For now, this isolated instant, Stacy felt secure within the confines of Main's strong embrace and reassuring murmurs. The release of rigidly contained grief was exhausting, and closing her eyes, Stacy rested her head against the solid wall of his chest. Gulping deep, uneven breaths, she drew in the scent of him—spicy, clean, musky and all male—so different from the smell of pipe tobacco, unscented shaving soap and sun-dried clothing she associated with her grandfather, yet somehow just as calming and soothing.

Stacy was lulled by the mesmerizing effect of Main's hand stroking her hair, her back. A long sigh whispered through her lips as the storm of weeping subsided. His low voice washed over her like a healing balm.

"That's it. That's good. Rest now. You're tired. But it'll be all right. We'll make it right. Together."

"Together?" Stacy lifted her head and raised tear spiked lashes to gaze misty-eyed at him.

"Yes." Main smiled at her with infinite tenderness. "I'd offer to stay at a motel but, Lord, Stacy, I can't leave you alone here now. You look so damn vulnerable."

She sniffed and managed a watery smile. "I'm not, you know. I'm really very tough."

"Are you?" Main asked with a hint of skeptical indulgence. His gray eyes grew dark as storm clouds as he lowered his gaze to her trembling lips.

"Y-yes," Stacy had to force the word from her suddenly tight throat, for it was at that moment that awareness of him, as a man, a fully aroused man, flooded her senses.

"Stacy."

The low, ragged sound of his voice cut her breath off. Her eyes widened and fastened on his mouth as she watched him slowly lower his head to her. Stacy moved restlessly, indicating a desire to be set free. Too late.

Main's arms tightened, imprisoning her against his hard body. She gave a soft gasp as his mouth grazed hers.

"Don't." As protests went, Stacy's was weak sounding, without substance.

"I won't hurt you."

"Mr. Chance, I . . ."

"Main," he murmured, bringing a tantalizing tingle to the surface of her lips with another, lingering brush of his mouth over hers.

"Main." Stacy complied in a faint echo, feeling the resistance drain from her mind and body.

His mouth grazed hers once more, then settled to conform to the outline of her lips. Stacy felt her mind shut down and her senses speed up. Main's kiss was all hard male and soft enticement. He tasted of raisin pie and coffee and the answer to hidden, secret erotic fantasies.

Lost and helpless in the alluring sensuality of Main's beguiling kiss, Stacy wound her arms around his neck to anchor herself, her whirling senses, to the inducement of his strong, hungry mouth.

It was madness . . . but delicious madness. And for an endless moment, Stacy drifted, mindless and uncaring, in the warm cocoon of sensuality he wove with his kiss.

Sanity returned when Main pierced the silken web by slipping his tongue between her lips and gliding his hands to her hips to lift her up, into the blatant proof of his desire.

"No." Stacy's voice broke, tremulous but decisive from her tight throat. "Main . . . stop. Please."

The near panic in her voice dissipated the sensuous haze clouding Main's rational mind. Breath shuddering from his heaving chest, he released his crushing hold on her and stepped back, away from further temptation.

"You taste good, Stacy." Main's crooked smile revealed the fury still raging in his body. "Too damn good. As sweet as cold mountain water on a blistering hot day."

Stacy could do no more than stare at him in wonderment, shaken to her depths by her response to him and the sensations his kiss had generated inside her.

"Is an apology in order?"

"What?" she asked, lost to comprehension in the heated gray universe of his eyes.

A knowing smile kicked up the corners of his mouth. "I asked if an apology was in order?"

"Oh!" Stacy blinked herself back to earth and shook her head. "No."

"That's good." Main grinned. "For I sure as hell would be lying if I told you I was sorry for kissing you. In all honesty, sweetheart, I haven't enjoyed anything half as much in a very long time."

"Don't call me sweetheart," Stacy admonished him, unwilling to reveal how pleased she felt from his compliment. Feeling her cheeks grow warm, she turned away, equally unwilling to have him see the evidence of her confusion and pleasure. "I don't appreciate casual endearments."

"I'm sorry to hear that," he observed in a serious, somber tone. "I kinda like the taste of it on my lips.

Saying the word *sweetheart,* savoring the flavor of it in my mouth, is almost as good as kissing you.''

Stacy's lips tingled at the teasing reminder. "Don't say things like that!" She whirled to confront him, and immediately wished she hadn't. His smoky eyes retained wisps of sensuous clouds, promising untold delights. And in that instant, an echo of his taunting voice, and her own defiant reply, whispered insidiously in her mind.

*Believe me, if I ever touch you*—meaningfully *touch you*—*you will know, and appreciate, the difference.*

*Dream on, Texan. You will never, and I repeat,* never *again get the opportunity to touch me*—*meaningfully or any other way.*

The echoes mocked Stacy. The Texan had advanced way beyond dreaming, and she had been helpless against his assault. He said something. She started.

"What?"

"I asked you why I shouldn't say 'things like that' when they are true." His voice was soft, low, a sexy inducement to her to abandon restraint.

Stacy felt an inner softening, an unfamiliar loosening that scared the hell out of her. "Because I don't like it," she lied, fighting him, and herself.

"But I like kissing you." Main smiled.

Stacy gulped. Suddenly desperate to move, change the subject, she blurted out, "I think I better go see if Anne needs help. It's soon quitting time for her."

"I'll trail along," Main offered. "If you don't mind?" He was openly laughing at her. "Then, after Anne leaves, you can give me the grand tour of the grounds and the house."

# Eight

"It's so green, so beautiful."

"Yes," Stacy murmured in response to Main's quietly voiced observation.

They were seated side by side on the porch steps, watching the sun make a last glorious retreat before the encroachment of evening. The golden sheen of the long rays bathed the land in a gentle, softening glow.

Stacy was grateful for the opportunity to sit and rest for a few minutes. She felt more tired than she usually did after working alongside Anne on a normal day.

She and Main had arrived at the stables as Anne was preparing to bring the animals in from the pastures. Working together, the three of them had quartered the time usually required to accomplish the task. To Stacy's astonishment, Main had worked right beside them throughout the entire process of bedding the animals down for the night. He helped muck out stalls, scatter clean hay and lug fresh feed and water.

After Anne had left for the day, Stacy had conducted Main on his requested tour of the property. To her mind, the word *examination* better suited the exercise.

Main's interest in everything had been comprehensive—to say the least. He had inspected every item in minute detail, beginning with the animals and ending with the equipment. And he had fired questions at Stacy all the while.

"She's a real beauty!" he'd exclaimed over Morning Star. "A true Thoroughbred from that small star-shaped blaze on her forehead to the tip of her silky tail."

"Yes." Stacy's chest swelled with pride and sheer love for the beautiful animal. "She's my favorite. My pet. Mine. She was my last birthday gift from my grandfather."

"Are you going to show her? Race her?"

"Not race her, no. But show her? I don't know. I've thought about it, but I haven't decided." Stacy sighed. "I haven't had the time to give any serious consideration to training her for dressage. I've been too busy."

"Doing what?"

Stacy bristled, at his tone as well as his question. "Trying to keep the place running, in addition to straightening my grandfather's desk," she retorted. "It hasn't been a picnic, you know. For some months now, I've been putting in sixteen-to-eighteen-hour days."

Main frowned, but she rushed on to explain without giving him a chance to ask another question.

"My grandfather always had three employees, a full-time trainer and groom and a part-time helper. He let the full-time men go when he sold over half his stock." She drew a ragged breath. "He had tried to run the place with the part-time man, who by the way, was almost as old as my grandfather."

"But surely you could see . . ."

"No, I couldn't!" Stacy cut him off with mounting irritation and impatience. "I told you I was living and working in Reading—not far in actual distant miles, but sizable in available commuting time, considering my erratic work schedule. I rarely had two consecutive days off. I visited my grandfather as often as I could, but I also had personal things to see to on my free time."

"I'm not condemning you, Stacy."

"You don't have to," she returned. "I did a good job of that myself." She heaved another deep sigh. "He sold the stock sometime last May, not quite a year ago, and appeared to be doing all right with the part-time man. But then, near the end of August, I arranged a long, four-day weekend, to spend some real time with him. I was shocked when I arrived. There was noticeable neglect of the property but, more important to me, were the unmistakable signs of my grandfather's failing health. I immediately quit my job, and after working a short notice, came home to stay. I didn't even have two full months with my grandfather before he died."

Talking about it resurrected the pain. Determining not to let her sense of loss engulf her again, Stacy went on grimly, "I've been playing catch-up ever since, so you see, I haven't had the time to think straight, let alone the opportunity to devote exclusively to training Morning Star." She didn't offer the additional information that she was sick from the very real possibility of having to sell her pet to acquire the working capital she desperately needed to keep going.

"You can begin soon," was all Main said, moving away from her to go to the far end of the stable.

Advice or a promise? Pondering the intent in his assertion, Stacy trailed after him.

"A magnificent Westphalian," Main softly praised when he at last came to the stallion's stall. Raising his hand he stroked Hammerhead's soft, nuzzling nose.

"You do know horses," she responded, impressed by his instant recognition of the breed. "Don't you?"

"I've always been interested in them," he said, flashing a smile at her that went directly to her senses. "I learned to ride when I was a kid."

"Your family owned horses?"

Main shook his head. "No. As a matter of fact, I'm the only member of my family who can ride." His smile was wry. "Maybe I'm a throwback."

Stacy was baffled and curious. "A throwback? I don't understand. In what way?"

"My grandfather was a genuine working cowboy."

The light dawned in Stacy's mind. "The man my grandfather's stepsister eloped with." Although she hadn't posed it as a question, Main answered anyway.

"Apparently."

As they conversed, Main systematically examined every mare and foal on the place. Watching his minute inspection with absent attention, Stacy murmured, "It would seem that it sometimes works that way."

Main drew his intent gaze from the fetlock of the mare he was in the process of examining, and stared at her with a blank, uncomprehending look. "It would seem that *what* sometimes works that way?"

"The throwback theory."

"Huh?" Forgetting the mare now nudging his shoulder for attention, Main turned to squarely face her. "You've lost me again, sweetheart."

"I asked you not to call me sweetheart," Stacy said, automatically and without emphasis. "And what I meant was that the throwback tendency seems to occur frequently," she went on to explain. "I'm one myself."

"Really?" Main raised one quizzical brow.

"Hmm." Stacy murmured, nodding. "My father made it clear at a young age that he had no interest in the farm." A sad smile curved her soft mouth. "As a matter of fact, neither my father nor my mother liked horses very much."

Main's sharpened gray gaze sketched the downward curve of her lips. "Where are your parents now?" he asked with gentle perception.

A tremor skimmed across her mouth. "They're gone."

"I'm sorry." Though soft, his voice contained genuine sympathy.

"So am I." Stacy exhaled a long breath. "They were both so full of the joy of life and adventure."

"Adventure?" Main probed.

Stacy's eyes clouded with remembered pain. She was no longer aware of her surroundings; she didn't hear the restless shuffling of the horses, was unaware of the familiar mingled scents of the stables, the smell of animals and hay and leather.

"My father was a flight enthusiast." Her voice was barely audible in the darkening interior. "He piloted his own small charter plane. I... he and Mother were on vacation. They wanted to explore the West. A sudden storm erupted." She closed her eyes and swallowed; it burned her throat, the memories seared her mind. There were no tears. Over time, the searing pain had subsided to a dull ache. "The rescue team found the wreckage and—" she paused to swallow once more; still her voice had a dry, cracked quality "—and their bodies where the plane crashed into the side of a mountain."

"Stacy."

Suddenly, for the second time that afternoon, Stacy found herself enveloped in Main's comforting embrace. The scent of him overwhelmed her, making her light-headed, uncertain. She was so tired, and he felt so good, that all she wanted was to rest against him, inhaling and absorbing the mesmerizing masculine aura of him.

Giving in to weariness, and her weakness against his allure, Stacy allowed herself the luxury of his warm strength for a few precious seconds before shaking off his lightly encircling arms and stepping back, out of harm's way.

"Are you all right?"

"Yes," she answered, retreating from the clear note of concern in his voice. "It happened over six years ago, while I was still in college."

Main pursued her, and the conversation, from the stables. "You have no other family?"

Coming to a halt in the cooling air, Stacy gave a loud, long-suffering sigh as she whirled to face him. "I have a brother. He lives in California now. Like our parents, he also is not particularly fond of horses, which, I believe, was another reason Gramps sold off over half the stock. He wanted my brother to have his fair share." Her voice was rough, defensive. "Any other questions?"

Main smiled. "About a hundred thousand," he'd drawled. "But they can wait until later."

"What does your brother do?"

*It must be later.*

Swallowing a sigh, Stacy turned to level a wry look at him. "You don't quit, do you?"

Main laughed and shook his head in answer.

The sound of his soft laughter danced over every inch of her skin like a teasing feather. Stacy groaned. It wasn't fair for any one man's laughter to sound so beguiling and contain such will-corroding power.

Her throat was dry; her palms were moist. "He's a computer freak." Stacy despaired of the crack in her voice. "He designs programs."

"Impressive," he murmured, looking as though he meant it. "He must be pretty intelligent."

"He is," she said, jumping up and heading for the door. "Do you want to look over the house now or have supper first?'' She glanced back at him and immediately wished she hadn't. Merely watching him rise did a number on her senses.

Jasper Chance didn't simply stand up, like other men; he rose with a grace of movement that was fascinating in its sensuous fluidity.

Stacy was forced to swallow once more, this time to dislodge a tight fullness in her throat. Intent on dragging her gaze from his demoralizing appeal, she missed the beginning of his answer to the question she'd already forgotten.

''...and then I can see the rest of the house,'' he was saying, the tone of his voice and his walk lazy, as he crossed the porch to her.

Feeling stalked, Stacy pulled open the screen door and bolted into the kitchen. ''I...ah, I'm sorry.'' Her heart gave a little thump when the door swung shut with a definite, final-sounding click—not unlike what she imagined a closing animal trap or cell door might sound like.

''Sorry?'' He came to an abrupt stop and frowned. ''Sorry about what?''

Pull yourself together—you nit! Stacy chided herself, offering him a weak smile. ''I was...ah, thinking about something else. I didn't hear the first part of what you said.''

Though Main gave her a strange look, he didn't comment on her odd behavior. ''I said I'd really like a shower first, then dinner and then a tour of the house.'' He arched his brows. ''If you have no objections?''

A shower? Stacy swallowed. An ordinary request, certainly, after working in the stables. And yet, his request for a shower renewed and underscored his stated intention to stay the night, or many nights, at the farm. Under the circumstances, the ordinary request for a shower lent a hint of intimacy to the situation.

He had only been there for half a day, and already Stacy had felt herself melting in his embrace—not once but twice! What could she expect if he stayed...*slept* in the house? Her spine tingled, scaring her into clamping a lid on her overactive imagination, and putting on a front of bravado.

"No, I have no objections," she lied, pulling off a reasonable facsimile of a careless shrug. "I'll show you to the guest room and you can shower while I start dinner."

Main was moving to the door before she'd finished speaking. "I'll get my bag."

They sat down a little while later to a simple casserole and tossed salad.

"This is very good," Main said, digging into his food with gusto. "What did you call it?"

"Shepherd's pie." Stacy made a face. "Don't tell me you've never heard of it before?"

"I've never heard of it before," he said facetiously. "Other than grilled rare and served with sautéed onions on a bun, I've never been wild about hamburger meals," he admitted. "But this combination of hamburger, gravy and mashed potatoes is really very tasty. I like it."

"It's more of what Edith calls 'chust good, plain, stick-to-the-ribs fare'," Stacy said, mimicking the older woman's Pennsylvania Dutch accent.

"It is that." Main grinned. "I have a hunch that I'd better be careful. The food here is too good. Many more meals like I've had today and I'll have to go on a diet."

Right. Stacy kept her opinion to herself, while skimming an unobtrusive glance over what she could see of his lean torso above the tabletop. But aside from the question of weight, his assertion reinforced his determination to reside in the house.

As if his determination needed reinforcement! After making up the bed in the guest room and nearly tripping over the duffel bag he had dropped at the foot of the bed, the last thing Stacy needed was reinforcement of his determination.

*Duffel bag!*

The startled thought reverberated inside Stacy's mind. Main couldn't have more than one or two changes of clothes in that small bag.

Maybe... just maybe, he wasn't serious about staying on indefinitely. The prospect had an odd, conflicting effect on Stacy. Unwilling to delve into her waffling feelings, she pushed them aside in favor of quizzing him.

"Is that one duffel bag the only piece of luggage you have with you?"

"Yeah, but don't get your hopes up, sweetheart," Main repeated his earlier advice.

Had it really only been hours since he'd given her the same advice? It seemed like days, weeks, months. Stacy was so bemused by the realization that she already felt she had known him for ages, she didn't even bother telling him not to call her sweetheart.

"You're planning on making do with a couple of changes of clothing?" Without giving him time to respond, she went on, "Or were you planning on trying to talk me into doing laundry for you everyday?"

"I am capable of doing my own laundry," Main retorted with a chiding smile. "But, no, I wasn't planning on either. I'll only be here until Monday morning."

Stacy nearly choked on the food she was in the process of swallowing. "Monday!" she exclaimed after taking a sip of water to wash down the food. "You're leaving on Monday?"

"Yes," he confirmed in a silky tone. "But don't start doing cartwheels for joy just yet. I'll be back."

"Oh," Stacy muttered, asking herself why she didn't feel a sense of disappointment.

What had happened to all her previous feelings of anger, resentment and indignation?

"I have some things to take care of."

"Things?" she repeated blankly, corralling her introspective thoughts. "What things?"

The look he gave her said clearly that the answer should be obvious. Nevertheless, he proceeded to explain. "I have to collect my belongings, see my lawyer, visit my banker, tie up loose ends...those things."

See his lawyer and visit his banker! "You really are thinking of making this your permanent residence, aren't you?" she blurted out in surprise.

"Didn't I tell you I was?"

"Yes...but..."

"I knew I heard it somewhere," Main wryly drawled when her voice faded away.

"But you can't!" Stacy cried. "I mean, I know you have the legal right to move in, but..."

"There are no buts, Stacy," Main interrupted her. "I like what I've seen of the property, and since half of it is mine, I intend to claim it, live on it."

"Then I'll have to move." Stacy reiterated her earlier decision. "I can't live here alone with you."

"That's ridiculous." Impatience flickered across his face and sharpened his voice.

"Is it?" Stacy asked, staring dully at the now empty plates on the cluttered table. "I don't think so."

"Well, I do." Main scowled. "Dammit, Stacy, we're adults, we can figure out a working arrangement."

Sighing, she stood and began stacking the plates. "What did you have in mind?" she asked, slamming the plates onto the table and glaring at him. "Were you thinking of sectioning off the place, maybe cutting the house in half?"

Main had the unmitigated gall to laugh in her face. "Now you are being ridiculous."

"So, all right, I'm ridiculous!" Stacy shouted, giving in to the weariness and mixed emotions playing hell with her mind. "And I'm probably old-fashioned and out of step with the current mores, whatever they are." Snatching up the dishes once more, she stormed to the sink. Her hands had a noticeable tremor as she turned on the tap and rinsed the plates in the flow of hot water. "So...sue me." Her voice was tight with defiance, her movements jerky as she yanked open the dishwasher door and began stacking the dishes into the racks.

"C'mon, Stacy." Main's chair grated against the floor and her nerves. "Calm down."

Calm down? Calm down! Stacy was hard-pressed not to laugh. Hysterically. How was she supposed to calm down with him closing in on her like an enveloping fog? He was right behind her. Dammit, she could smell him! The knives and forks slipped from her fingers, missed the basket and clattered onto the base of the dishwasher. Calm down? Hah! She was amazed she didn't fly apart at the seams.

"Are you . . . er, attached?"

Stacy frowned, in confusion and in response to the sensations caused by his warm breath ruffling her hair. His broad hand settled on her shoulder. She felt the effect of his touch to her curling toes.

Attached. How? Like, were her mental hinges secure?

"In what way?" she asked warily, inching around to face him. It was a mistake; Main was practically on top of her. Stacy could count the laugh lines radiating from the corners of his eyes. His deep, dark eyes. Her breath caught in a tight knot somewhere between her chest and her throat.

"In the usual way." Main stared into her eyes, as if trying to probe into her soul. "With a man."

"What do you mean?" Stacy asked, being deliberately obtuse, but needing to hear him spell it out.

His smile was sardonic. "Is there a special man in your life," he said bluntly. "One you sleep with?"

# Nine

"That's none of your damn business!" Stacy exclaimed, pushing away from the sink, and him.

"Under normal conditions, I'd agree," Main said, tracking her to the table. "But we're not operating under normal conditions." He cocked one brow. "Are we?"

Stacy applied the dishrag to the tabletop with more vigor than finesse. "Normal or not, I don't see what my sleeping arrangements have to do with it."

"Don't you?" Main's smile mocked her. "Are you telling me he won't object?"

"Who he?" Stacy groaned in silent frustration. "I mean, what he?" Oh, good grief!

Main laughed. "He…the man in your life," he said around a throaty chuckle. "Whoever he is."

"There is no . . . he!" Stacy heaved a sigh of self-disgust; she was getting more idiotic by the second.

"No?" His soft voice had the unmistakable sound of a contented purr.

The short hairs at Stacy's nape quivered. Straightening from her bent-over position at the table, she turned to give him a narrow-eyed, leery look. Main had the appearance of a big, well-fed barn cat.

"No," she said, steeling herself against the unsettling effects of his nearness. "There is no man."

"Why?"

Stacy's temper frayed. "That's also none of your business," she snapped.

"I know." Main shrugged. "But I'm curious."

"Try nosy."

"Okay. I'm nosy." He grinned. "Why?"

Her patience frayed along with her temper. "Because I'm not interested, that's why."

His dark eyebrows shot into a high arch. "I find that hard to believe."

Stacy shrugged. "Suit yourself."

"I usually do."

"This conversation's going nowhere," Stacy said, tossing the dishrag into the sink. "Do you want to see the rest of the house or not?"

"I do."

"Then let's get it over with." She marched past him. "I have more important things to do."

"Like what?" Main sauntered after her.

"Like take a shower," she shot back. "Or try to balance the books. Or twiddle my thumbs."

Main laughed then, ignoring her first and last cracks, homing in on the important one. "You're having difficulty balancing your books?"

"It's been known to happen when there's more outgo than income," she said sarcastically. "This is the dining room," she muttered, almost in the same breath. Not pausing to stop, she headed for the connecting archway. "And this is the living room," she went on, indicating with a sweeping motion of her hand the spotless, comfortable-looking room.

"Nice."

"Thank you. I decorated it for my grandfather. I may even get a minute to sit down in here someday." She kept moving, into the long hallway that connected the kitchen to the front foyer. "From here on in, you're on your own." Dismissing the living room, and him, she made for the narrow staircase. "You've seen the upstairs. I'm going to have a shower."

"You're a lousy hostess," Main called up the stairs after her in a laughing voice.

"Tough nuggies," she retorted.

"Nuggies?"

His deep-throated bark of laughter chased Stacy along the second-floor hallway and into her bedroom.

"Nuggies," Main repeated the word between breaths still uneven with laughter. What a dumb expression, he mused, shaking his head as he took the short route through the long hallway back to the kitchen.

Dumb, maybe, but effective. Main hadn't a clue to its definition, but he got the meaning and message intended. Stacy was telling him that she didn't give a rip what he thought of her as a hostess...or anything else.

But she would...and soon.

Grinning as his battle plan formed in his mind, Main crossed to the sink and set about finishing the cleanup job Stacy had left half done.

So, there was no man in her life.

Good.

That's all Main needed to know. From here on, he knew he had the ammunition to shoot down any and all objections she had in her arsenal to launch in a counterattack.

A thought struck Main that made him laugh out loud.

*He'd pull a "Desert Storm" on Stacy—dazzle her with his smart verbal bombs, and then out flank her with logic!*

Pleased with his plan of attack, and himself, Main gathered the last of the utensils from the dishwasher base, dumped them into the basket, locked the door and switched on the washer, then turned to go in search of the one room Stacy had omitted from the downstairs tour.

Main found the door to the small office at the far end of the dining room, opposite the archway into the living room.

No wonder she went through the dining room like a dose of salts, he reflected, smiling wryly as he tested the knob with a tentative twist. The door was not locked. The knob turned smoothly and the door swung open.

The desk positioned in the corner between two long windows had to be an antique, and was probably beautiful—if one could find it beneath the cluttered pile of papers, folders, ledgers and current and back issues of horse publications.

"What a mess," Main muttered, dropping into the high-backed swivel chair and drawing it up to the desk. "Oh, well," he went on talking to himself, "I've nothing better to do until my hostess returns and hostilities break out." Heaving a sigh, he reached for the top ledger.

While Main grumbled in the office, Stacy was doing her own muttered grousing a floor above.

"Outdoorsy, pine and..." She sniffed the redolent scent lingering on the bathroom air. "Sage?" She sniffed again, catching the dissipating aromas of masculine soap, shaving cream and after-shave splash.

The heady fragrance saturated Stacy's senses, tingled along her nerve endings and caused a fine tremor in her fingers and, of all places, her thighs.

Memory stirred, recent memory, of Main strolling into the kitchen after his shower. Even dressed in casual slacks and cotton pullover wrinkled by too many hours stuffed into a duffel bag, he looked and smelled good enough to eat with a spoon.

"Smells delicious," he'd murmured, breathing in the aromatic steam rising from the casserole and warm dinner rolls.

"Yes," she'd responded, breathing in the aromatic warmth radiating from his clean body.

Drat the man!

How long had it been since she'd noticed the distinctive scent of a man? Stacy mused, turning the taps and adjusting the water temperature. She frowned. Had she ever noticed any man's personal scent? Other than her grandfather's—and that was hardly the same—offhand, she couldn't recall having done so. Not even Dan's.

Strange, she reflected, stepping into the tub and drawing the curtain. Very strange that the only scent that had ever aroused her awareness belonged to Jasper Chance.

Stacy had not planned to take the time to wash her hair but, under such adverse conditions, one was forced to fight fire with stronger fire. After stepping beneath the seething shower spray, she squeezed a liberal amount of jasmine-scented shampoo into her palm and worked it vigorously into her sodden locks. Following the shampoo, she lathered her slick body generously with a bar of white ginger-scented soap.

Unfortunately, the countering measure failed miserably; his scents and her scents blended into one powerful and enticingly erotic imagination teaser.

Feeling her fragrance-drenched mind skipping along the way of all fleshly pursuits, Stacy muttered a curse, stepped from the shower, and barely taking time to conceal her dripping wet body with a bath sheet, fled the seductive odors permeating the steamy bathroom.

Stacy had herself under tight control when at last she was ready to leave the safety of her bedroom to again face her uninvited houseguest.

She was dressed for comfort rather than impression in close-fitting, stone-washed jeans, a long-sleeved soft cotton white shirt and flat ballerina-style house slippers. Her long hair, still damp in spots from her hasty use of the blow dryer, was again anchored at her nape with a simple gold-tone hair clip. The only concession Stacy had made to company in the house was the wisp of color applied to her cheeks with the swish of the blush brush and the glide of pink lipstick to her mouth.

Twilight was fast giving way to full darkness. Moving along the dim hallway, Stacy paused, then came to a full stop beside the clothes hamper positioned outside the bathroom.

With her own words of a short time ago mocking her actions, Stacy flipped up the hamper lid and pulled her and Main's soiled clothing from the container and dumped them into the laundry basket sitting on the floor next to the hamper.

Balancing the basket against her hip, she moved to the far end of the hallway, to the back stairs that led directly into the kitchen.

The room was dark and cool. Setting the basket onto the floor, Stacy flicked on the bright overhead light, then went to close the solid door against the chill of the early-spring night breeze.

Where the devil was he?

"Main?"

Stacy scooped up the basket and made for the laundry room off the kitchen. She separated the clothes into color piles then, gingerly picking up his shockingly brief underpants, tossed them into the machine along with the other whites. She then poured in the liquid detergent, shut the lid and pushed the start button. That part of the chore completed, Stacy went in search of Main.

She found him in the one room she had deliberately not shown him. Main was seated at her grandfather's oak desk, poring over one of the leather-bound ledgers.

"Interesting reading?" Though soft, her tone of voice carried a definite barb.

Main raised his head and turned to her, his gray eyes dark with contemplation and concern. "I knew breeding horses was expensive, but I had no idea how very expensive."

"Upward of twenty thousand a year per horse," Stacy said. "And I do mean upward."

"So I see." Main tapped the ledger with the tip of one finger. "As with everything else, prices are spiraling. You really are in a financial bind, aren't you?"

Stacy bristled, but bit back an angry retort for him to mind his own business. In truth, the financial situation of the farm was every bit as much his business as her own.

"I did tell you that money was tight," she reminded him, swallowing the acrid taste of impending disaster. "I'm hanging on by my teeth."

Main glanced back at the ledger, shook his head, then returned his laser stare to her closed expression. "How in hell were you hoping to survive?"

Taking umbrage to what she assumed was a note of censure in his astonished tone, Stacy glared at Main in glittery-eyed, tight-lipped silence.

"Dammit, Stacy, answer me! I have a right to know." Main exploded in response to her resistant attitude. "Were you planning on selling off more stock, some of the land, or mortgaging the property?"

"No, no and no!" Stacy erupted.

"Then what?" He shot another look at the ledger. "Good Lord, woman, you're down to your last couple of thousand dollars! You've got an unpaid account with Dan, and overdue bills with the feed store and tack shop." He ruffled his newly washed, neatly brushed hair with long raking fingers. "You need at least two more employees, and you can hardly afford to pay Anne's salary now." He drew a harsh breath that spoke reams about exasperation. "Talk to me, Stacy! How were you hoping to continue operating this way?"

Stacy broke under pressure of months of worry and work and pure, unmitigated fear.

"I don't know!" She drew a deep breath, and then another. It didn't help; she still felt as though she were suffocating. Her voice betrayed the closing of her throat. "Other than to sell Morning Star, I...I just...don't know."

Main was on his feet with a blur of motion, the desk chair tipping precariously from the swiftness of his action.

"For Christ's sake, sweetheart!" he exclaimed in a soft, startled growl. "You have the look of someone becoming unglued. I think you'd better sit down before you fall down." Grasping her upper arms, he steered her to the only other chair in the room, a big leather recliner.

"I'm all right." Stacy's automatic protest lacked both substance and conviction.

"Yeah, and I'm Peter Pan," he retorted.

Stacy laughed; she couldn't help it. Despite a slight sensation of light-headedness and the heavy weight of weariness, she couldn't help making a comparison between the tall, whipcord tough-looking man looming over her and the small, skinny, forever young boy of fictional fantasy. Of course, there was absolutely no comparison between Main and Peter Pan. That's why she had to laugh.

"You're losing it, sweetheart." Main's narrowed gaze raked her pale face, then probed the depths of her eyes, as if searching out the secrets of her soul.

"I assure you I am not." Stacy gave a quick, hard shake of her head. "And don't call me sweetheart," she said, pushing at the hands he had planted on the chair arms on either side of her, caging her.

"You always laugh hysterically?" His smile was chiding but gentle... almost tender.

Stacy's breath did its suffocating routine once more, partly in response to his smile, but mostly in reaction to the way he hunkered down in front of her.

"No, I..." Her voice cracked and she was forced to swallow to moisten her parched throat and wet her lips with a darting glide of her tongue.

His intent gaze fastened onto her mouth. "You'll wash the lipstick away doing that, sweetheart."

Stacy's heart gave a funny, painful little thump. He was too close, too masculine, too...

"I asked you not to call me sweetheart," she muttered, dragging her gaze, and her thoughts, away from the overpowering sensual enticement of him.

"And I told you that I like the sound of it, the taste of it in my mouth." His darkening gaze flicked to her eyes, then back to her lips. "It reminds me of the sexy, exciting and arousing taste of you."

"Don't." Stacy's voice was weak, a true reflection of her dwindling resistance to his allure. Fighting a sudden wild impulse to lean forward to close the scant distance separating her mouth from his, she pressed back into the butter-soft leather of the chair.

"Don't?" Main softly repeated, instilling amazement and an unmistakable thrill in Stacy by surging forward, practically covering her slender form with his body. "Don't... what?" he asked in a soft purr, bathing her lips with his warm breath, and her already undermined senses with his spicy scent.

Stacy's breath came to a dead stop. She wet her lips again, then withdrew the tip of her tongue when he slowly mirrored her unconscious act of seduction.

"Don't... anything." Her voice came in short, gasping puffs. "Please."

"Ahh...sweetheart, take pity." Main moved closer, and still closer, until his mouth was less than a quick breath from hers. "I want to kiss you so bad, my teeth hurt."

"No." As rejections went, Stacy's was miles from convincing—either him or herself.

She wanted his mouth. It was as simple, and unraveling, as that.

"You said we must talk," she whispered in a rush, denying her burning lips the healing balm of his mouth.

"We will." Closer still he came, tantalizing her with the promise of contact.

"Wh-when?"

"After I've kissed you."

"Main, please."

"Please kiss you?" His mouth brushed against hers with electrifying effect.

"Yes," she murmured in temporary insanity and momentary surrender.

"Yes," he breathed, fitting his mouth to the contours of her trembling lips.

Stacy braced herself for an onslaught of sensual demands that didn't materialize. Instead of a display of hot urgency, Main revealed warm restraint.

His kiss was gentle, tender, infinitely sweet, spinning a soothing cocoon of comfort around her uprooted emotions and battered feelings.

A wayward tear escaped one tightly closed eyelid, swiftly followed by another, to glide down her cheek and splash onto the big hand lightly cradling her face.

Main suddenly shifted position, and her, until they were lying side by side on the wide, man-size chair. His fingers crept to the source of the moisture, and stroked across her spiky lashes.

"Don't cry, Stacy," he murmured into her mouth. "Everything will be all right."

"But—" Stacy had to pause to sniff "—you've seen the books and... oh, Main, I'm so afraid I'll have to give up Morning Star, and still lose it all."

"No you won't," he crooned, bestowing the blessing of another soft kiss. "You'll see."

"But..."

"Hush, now." His voice was a low caress in her ear, his lips a benediction to her tremulous mouth. "You're tired. You need rest, sleep."

Stacy moved fretfully, breaking the soothing contact with his undemanding lips. "I can't rest," she cried. "And I haven't been able to sleep through one entire night since Gramps died." A shudder of exhaustion flowed through the length of her body. "I don't know what to do anymore."

"I do." Main said with quiet conviction, working his arms around her to cradle her close to his own hard strength. "I told you everything will be all right."

"I don't see how," Stacy argued. "As you were quick to point out, I'm running out of money."

"I'm not."

Stacy sighed and angled her head to look up, into his calm gray eyes. "I can't take money from you."

His eyes flickered, instantly changing from calm to stormy. "We'll talk about it tomorrow," he said with just a hint of impatience. "After you've had some rest."

Stacy sniffed and lifted her chin. "No. We'll talk about it now. I cannot, *will* not take money from you."

The corner of his mouth twitched. "But you forget," he chided, "I own half the place. You can't stop me from investing in it."

Stacy's defiance deflated like a punctured balloon. "Oh, why did Gramps do this?" she whispered harshly. "It's not fair! It's not even proper."

"Oh, you want proper?" Main's tone was smooth, silky, too smooth, too silky.

"Yes!" Stacy exclaimed, too distracted to notice his tone of voice, or the strange stillness of his body.

"Then there's only one thing we can do."

Hope flared to life inside Stacy, the hope that he was finally ready to concede to the impossible situation they now found themselves caught in—concede and withdraw. "What are you suggesting?" she asked, with cautious eagerness.

"I think we should get married."

# Ten

―――――

"**M**arried!"

Rearing back in astonishment, Stacy leapt from the chair like a bee-stung cat.

"Yes, married," Main replied with infuriating calm. Shifting onto his back, he folded his arms under his head and smiled at her. "Seems the rational thing to do."

"Rational?" Stacy yelped. "It's the least rational, most insane idea I've ever heard!" She gasped for air, and silently prayed that she wouldn't hyperventilate.

"Why?"

"Why?" she sputtered. "I . . . I'll tell you why. We don't even know each other, for one thing!"

"What does that have to do with it?"

Stacy gaped at him. "It has everything to do with it. For pity's sake, we only just met."

Main shrugged. "I've always heard that, no matter how long a man and woman know each other, they don't really *know* each other until they have lived together." He arched one eyebrow. "Haven't you heard that old saw?"

"Yes, of course, but—"

"There you go," he cut in smoothly. "If that's the case, what's the difference if we've known each other for a dozen years, or since lunchtime today?"

"One of us is a little crazy," she said, backing away from him. "And I don't believe it's me." Reaching the door, she kept a wary eye on him and groped for the knob.

Main watched with implacable calm as she fumbled to open the door. "Where are you going?" He frowned when she finally managed to complete the task and began backing from the room.

"Ah...I put a load of clothes in the washer before I came in here," she said, taking another backward step into the dining room. "I have to transfer it into the dryer." Before she had finished speaking, she spun and made a headlong dash through the kitchen and into the laundry room.

Incipient panic clawed at Stacy's throat. Her breathing was erratic; her thoughts chaotic.

Marriage! The man wasn't merely a little crazy...he was a raving lunatic! And she was alone in the house with him. And it was dark. What did that have to do with it? Dark, light, what difference did it make? The bright light of afternoon hadn't deterred him from kissing her before. And she had felt the hunger rising in him then.

Oh, without doubt, she would give him a good fight if he tried anything funny, Stacy staunchly reassured herself. But she was wise enough to realize that inevitably, in the end, he'd easily overcome her resistance, and then...

"What are you doing, standing out here in the dark?" Main's quiet voice broke into her wildly racing thoughts with the effect of a loud explosion.

Stacy gave a muffled scream and whirled around to face him, her hands raised defensively.

"For God's sake, Stacy, loosen up," Main snapped, taut impatience in his voice and movements as he flipped the wall switch, bathing the room in sudden bright light. "What's with you, anyway?"

Stacy kept her hands up, palms toward him. "Don't...don't you dare touch me."

"Touch you?" First he frowned; then he laughed. "Touch you!" His roar of laughter bounced off the walls of the small room. "I don't believe this," Main chortled. "I don't believe you!" The humor fled from his eyes as he stared at her stark expression. "You can relax, sweetheart. I'm not going to jump your bones."

"You're not?" Stacy couldn't decide if she felt relieved or insulted. The emotional uncertainty threw her off balance. "Why not?" she unthinkingly blurted out.

"Why not?" Main gave her a patently false look of innocence. "Why, we hardly know each other." His eyes reflected his inner amusement. "But if you insist...." He stepped forward, bringing his chest into contact with her hands.

"No!" Stacy felt his body heat through the smooth material of his knit pullover. Feeling singed, she snatched her hands away and retreated. "I didn't mean..." Her voice failed as her hips collided with the washer.

"Got you trapped," he murmured, leering with evil intent. "What are you going to do about it?"

"I...I'll scream," Stacy warned, fighting an impulse to giggle at the exaggerated contortion of his mouth.

"Hammerhead to the rescue?"

Stacy lost it. Her laughter peeled out, defusing the tension simmering between them. "You *are* crazy!" she choked out between gasps for breath.

Main appeared crestfallen. "Are you insinuating that I'll never make it as a classic villain?"

"I haven't decided if you'll make it till tomorrow," she retorted, controlling her mirth. "All that talk about marriage could bring you to a bad end."

His expression sobered in a flash.

What in hell did he think he was doing? Main upbraided himself. Well, he knew what he was doing. He was crowding Stacy, outflanking her.

That wasn't according to plan. His original idea was to soften Stacy up with his superior verbal smart bombs, then outflank her with logic.

Back it up, Chance, before you screw it up, Main advised himself, literally backing away from Stacy.

"I was serious about marriage," he said, keeping his voice low and calm, so as not to further upset her.

"Don't start that again!" Stacy muttered, turning to lift the lid of the machine.

"But I think it will work," he said with soft insistence. "Will you at least hear me out?"

Stacy was pulling underwear and towels from the washer and firing them into the dryer at a furious pace. Without breaking or as much as slowing her rhythm, she snapped, "Oh, all right! Say your piece and get it over with."

Women! Why did they always have to be so difficult? Exhaling to release the irritation building inside him, Main counted to ten before replying.

"Could we possibly have a reasonable discussion?" he asked in a controlled tone. "Face-to-face?"

The dryer door shut with a resounding bang. "Okay." Stacy pushed the start button, then whipped around. "We're face-to-face. But I think it's only fair to warn you that my reasonableness is on a short rein."

"There's a shocker."

Stacy scowled at the drawling sound of his voice. "Do you want to play straight man or talk?"

"Here?" Main's eyebrows shot into a taunting arch as he glanced around the tiny room. "Couldn't we go into the kitchen and sit down?"

Making a rude noise that sounded suspiciously like a snort, Stacy spun around once more, dumped detergent and the load of colored clothes into the washer, shut the lid, hit the start switch, then pivoted to once again face her tormentor.

He grinned at her.

Raising her eyes, Stacy addressed the ceiling. "Next thing you know, he'll be asking if I'd possibly be willing to fix him a snack and get him a cold beer."

"Would you?" Main's smile was designed to melt any and all objections. The design worked.

"Oh, all right," Stacy grumbled, pushing past him into the kitchen. "What do you want on your sandwich?"

"You make a mean sandwich, sweetheart." Polishing off the last of his sandwich with potato chips on the side, Main took a swig from his beer can and sat back in his chair, heaving a sigh of contentment.

Stacy waved the compliment aside and gave him a stern look. "Okay, talk... and don't call me sweetheart."

"I've already explained that I like the taste—"

"Talk!" Stacy ordered.

Main contrived a woeful, put-upon expression. "You're a hard woman, Stacy." He hesitated, a devilish gleam dancing in his darkening gray eyes. "Well, not really. In fact, you're soft, silky, supple...."

"That does it." Pushing her chair back, Stacy jumped up. "I'm going to bed."

"Ah, c'mon, Stace," Main groused, choking back laughter. "Where's your sense of humor?"

"I lost it somewhere before lunchtime today," she retorted, making for the stairs.

"Not true," he stated flatly. "If you're honest, you'll have to admit that we've laughed together several times since I arrived this morning."

What he claimed was true, they had shared moments of mutual laughter. But more than true, it was unusual, at least for the past few months. Stacy hadn't experienced many instances of sheer amusement since her grandfather's death.

"Will you come sit down if I promise to be good?" Main asked in a cajoling tone.

She paused at the back stairway to glance at him. His expression of tender understanding was her undoing. Undecided whether he could read her mind, or if she were that transparent, Stacy heaved a sigh of defeat and returned to the table—and Main.

"I can be very good, you know?" The teasing light in his eyes betrayed his somber mien.

"Don't push your luck, Chance."

"Spoilsport." He grinned, but held his hand up in the traditional sign of peace when she hesitated, her bottom inches from the chair seat. "Sit...please."

Stacy sat, but with obvious reluctance. "I really can't see the necessity for this discussion," she announced, propping her elbows on the table and her head in her hands. "Your suggestion is too ridiculous to be taken seriously."

"It isn't ridiculous," Main insisted. "Considering the circumstances, it makes perfect sense."

"But..."

"You're neither engaged nor involved." He interrupted without compunction. "Right?"

"Yes, but—" Stacy began again, only to have him interrupt her again.

"Is there any particular someone you have a hankerin' for?" he continued.

"A hankerin'? No." Stacy shook her head decisively. "There's no one."

"Same for me." Main lifted his shoulders in a light shrug. "So, then, why shouldn't we combine our inheritances, and forces, in marriage?"

"For one very good reason," Stacy came back at him. "I don't believe in marriage."

"As an institution?"

"No, personally." Stacy paused, then went on to explain, "I consider the dubious state of marital bliss to be nothing more than voluntary bondage for most women."

"No kidding?" Main didn't appear shocked, he looked rather reflective. "Interesting concept, and probably correct," he conceded. "But it doesn't apply in our case," he quickly pointed out. "That's the beauty of an arranged or, if you will, a marriage of convenience."

"A marriage of convenience for whom?" Stacy retaliated with sarcastic skepticism.

"For both of us, Stace." Main leaned forward over the table, his gaze intent on her.

"But I don't believe in marriage," Stacy repeated, more for herself than him.

"I don't believe in love," he retorted. "But what does that have to do with anything?"

"You don't believe in love?"

"Not the stars-in-the-eyes, romantic type—no." His eyes were clear, honest. "That's one of the reasons I believe my proposal is perfect."

"I'm afraid you've lost me." Stacy's expression reflected her mental state—utter blankness.

Ignoring the half-finished beer near his hand, Main explained. "You don't believe in marriage because you consider it a form of female bondage. I don't believe in romantic love because I consider it self-delusion. And that's the beauty of my plan. By entering into an arrangement like the one I have in mind, we both get to retain our beliefs. I won't expect you to answer to me for every decision you make, and you won't expect mushy, meaningless words of undying love from me. We'll be equal partners, not only in our business venture, but in a lifetime venture, as well. Now do you understand?''

"I suppose." Stacy nodded, but then hedged. "But as equal partners, what, exactly, would my contribution be to this business and lifetime venture?''

Now Main paused, and as though biding for time to gather his arguments—or courage—he picked up the can, examined the label and took a long swallow of the beer. Then he drew a deep breath and plunged.

"Children, for one.''

Stacy recoiled. Her spine slammed against the back of the chair. "Children? You mean you'd expect . . ." Her voice dried up, and she swallowed with visible difficulty.

"Join the real world, sweetheart," he advised in a chiding tone. "Of course I'd expect you to share my bed. I'm assuming we are both adults, with normal, healthy physical demands and appetites to be appeased." Main's laser stare bored into her surprise widened eyes. "But should you decide to enter into this agreement, you can be certain of one thing. I will never give you a moment of doubt about my fidelity. I give you my word here and now that I will honor the conditions of the agreement and my marriage vows until the day I die.''

Stacy's spine ached from being pressed against the hardwood. He was so intense, and sounded so sincere. She didn't know quite how to respond, what to say.

She'd have to share his bed, which meant she'd have to accept his body.

She shivered . . . not entirely with trepidation. "I . . . uh . . . you alluded to other contributions from me."

"Of course." Main eased back in his chair, as if resting after completing the worst hurdle. "Your expertise will be of equal value to the combined venture."

Her tired mind was grinding down to a slow stop. Stacy blinked. "My expertise?"

"Yes." Main gave her another of his sweet smiles of gentle understanding. "You have the business operational know-how, but lack funds. I have the funds, but lack the know-how. A fair exchange, I think. Don't you?"

"But you know horses. I saw you . . ."

"You saw my smattering of knowledge of horseflesh," he stated. "But, while it's true that I picked up a little experience of horses while I was managing the rental stable in West Texas, I have no experience at all in the business of breeding and training the animals." His smile tilted. "All I have is money—a lot of money."

All he had was money. Stacy suppressed a bubble of hysterical laughter. She rubbed her forehead. She felt taut with nerves. She was tired. Her head was beginning to pound, very likely because his proposal was beginning to not only make sense but to sound like the answer to her problems. But she could barely think coherently, let alone make a decision of such magnitude. She needed time and, more importantly, rest.

Sensing her uncertainty, Main pushed his advantage. "Look, Stace, we can hammer it all out between us, lay out the ground rules—down to the smallest detail. If it would make you feel easier or safer about the arrangement, we could even have contracts drawn up, covering all the conditions." He drew a deep breath. "What do you say?"

Stacy massaged her now throbbing temples. "Oh, I don't know. An arranged marriage. It's so...so..." She shrugged. "Besides, you don't have to marry me to invest in the business. Half of it's yours. You'd be investing in your own future."

"I don't only want to stay here, Stace," Main said, in a hard tone that contrasted sharply with the soft, pleading expression in his eyes. "I want to be a part of it...to belong. Will you at least give it some thought?"

Stacy sighed. "I'm tired."

"I know." Main smiled. "I won't badger you anymore tonight. Why don't you take a couple of aspirin and go to bed?"

The suggestion held infinite appeal, but Stacy sighed again. "I must finish the laundry."

"I'll do that." Main stood, then circled the table to urge her up. "And I'll clean up this mess after I've finished my beer." He drew her to her feet with a gentle touch and infinite care. "Go to bed, sweetheart."

"You're sure you don't mind?" Stacy asked, remembering her lessons on hostess behavior.

"If I'd minded, I wouldn't have offered." His smile grew a funny quirk. "And I promise, I'll handle your little lacy unmentionables with the utmost delicacy," he vowed, revealing to her that he had taken note of the dainty articles while she'd transferred the underwear to the dryer.

Despite her weariness, Stacy had to laugh. "You're all heart, Jasper Chance."

"Well..." he drawled. "...not *all* heart."

Stacy gave up, and fled for the back stairs.

As it had before, Main's laughter chased her all the way to her bedroom.

# Eleven

———

Stacy knew the moment she opened her eyes that it was late. The sun's rays glanced off her bedroom window, indicating a direct overhead rather than a slanting light.

She had overslept . . . way overslept!

And she hadn't even expected to get much sleep at all. Scrambling out of the rumpled bedcovers, Stacy recalled fearing she would toss and turn throughout the night, as she had done nearly every night since her grandfather died.

She had had a lot on her mind for months—worries about money, lack of enough help on the farm, money, the sudden information about a coheir, money. And now, adding to her sleep-robbing concerns, along came said coheir, issuing a mind-stopping, worry-increasing proposal.

No, Stacy had been positive she would not sleep last night. And so, naturally she'd gone out like a light the minute her head had hit the pillow, and not only had she slept through the night, but also halfway through a new day.

Pulling on her working garb of faded jeans, sweatshirt and well-worn boots, Stacy raked a brush through her hair, anchored the mass at her nape with a long barrette, then dashed for the bathroom to brush her teeth and splash water on her face. From the bathroom, she tore along the hallway and down the back stairs into the kitchen, fully expecting to find Main cooling his heels while impatiently waiting for her to make an appearance.

The room was empty.

Had Main overslept, as well?

A frown knitting her brows, Stacy skimmed a glance around the room, looking for some indication of him. She found it in the three-quarters full coffeepot, which was still hot. Main was not only up, but out . . . somewhere.

Where had he gone? she mused, standing next to the sink. Stacy mulled on Main's possible whereabouts as she vacillated between taking the time for a wake-up dose of caffeine and skipping the coffee to get right to work.

*Oh, bump the work!*

Stacy acted immediately on the rebellious thought by retrieving a cup from the cabinet above the sink and filling it with the steaming dark brew. Then, deciding that while she was at it she might as well go the whole route, she pulled a loaf of wheat bread from the bread drawer and dropped two slices into the toaster.

How did the British phrase it? she mused, collecting butter and a jar of strawberry preserves. In for a penny, in for a pound? Whatever. She was already late to the gate, so to speak. Besides, she was hungry.

Stacy was making inroads into her third piece of toast when Main strode across the porch and into the kitchen, sweaty and smelly from working in the stables. Even so, he looked better and more attractive than any other man she could recall at that moment. Somewhat rattled by his effortless effect on her senses, she gave him a wary look.

"What are you up to?"

Coming to a halt a few steps inside the screen door, Main raised a hand to the top of his head, then slid it out straight in midair and visually calculated the distance from his hand to the floor.

"Oh, 'bout six-four," he drawled.

"Cute." Stacy made a face and sank her teeth into the remaining piece of toast.

He laughed, and the sound wafted on the spring breeze to enfurl her, bringing a shiver to her spine and a reciprocal smile to her crumb-peppered lips. Stacy flicked her tongue out to collect the crumbs. Main's laughter abruptly ceased, and his laser gaze fastened on her mouth.

Stacy swallowed.

Main's gaze flickered to her throat.

Her heart gave a painful thump. Whoa! she thought, sitting very still to keep from squirming. The man was lethal.

"Uh...you've started cleaning the stables?" she said, while chiding herself for asking the obvious.

"No." He shook his head. "I've finished. The animals are all out and the stables are clean."

"But..."

"And I came in to invite you to lunch."

"Lunch?" Like a dimwit, Stacy shot a glance at her empty plate, then back to him.

"Yeah." Main shot a glance at the clock, then back to her. "It's the meal folks eat about this time of day."

"I just had breakfast."

Main shrugged. "So we'll wait an hour or two."

Stacy sat, just staring at him for a moment. Then her responsibilities as a hostess slammed into her. If he had completed the morning chores, he had very likely been at it for hours. He was probably hungry. Conscience-nudged, she jumped up, nearly knocking the chair over in her haste.

"I'll get you lunch," she offered, moving to the fridge. "What would you like?"

"You misunderstood," he said, halting her quick inventory of the interior of the fridge. "I said I came in to invite you to have lunch with me. Out...not here."

"Out? Where?" Stacy winced; she was still not exactly alert.

"Wherever." Main's smile held a hint of teasing. "I was hoping you'd give me a tour of the general area, stop to eat somewhere along the way."

"Oh." Stacy pondered his request for a moment, then recalled his aroused interest when Edith had mentioned Lititz. "Would you like to run over to Lititz?"

"Yeah." His eyes gleamed. "And Blue Ball. And Intercourse. And Ephrata. And Lancaster."

"Lank-uh-stir."

"Huh?"

Stacy laughed. "Around here, it's pronounced Lank-uh-stir, not Lang-kas-ter."

"It is?" Main's eyebrows arched.

"Umm." Stacy nodded. "It's like Greenwich."

He scowled. "Green-wich?"

"Exactly." She gave another brief nod. "Around here it's Green-wich, not Gren-ich."

"I see." His expression said the opposite. "Why?"

"How should I know?" She had to laugh again. "It's the way of the Pennsylvania Dutch . . . like Edith saying 'chust' for just." She shrugged. "Local accent."

"But you don't say 'chust.'"

"That's right." Stacy had difficulty keeping a straight face. "But I do say Lank-uh-stir."

"I give in."

"I thought you might."

"But I still want to go."

"Then go get cleaned up."

Main's lips twitched. "Are you insinuating I reek?"

"Chust a little."

Shaking his head, laughing all the way, Main strode for the back staircase.

A sudden memory flash propelled Stacy to the base of the stairs. "I can't go yet, Main," she called after him. "Dan said he'd stop by to check on Morning Star."

"He's been and gone," Main called back. "Said to tell you that Morning Star is fine, and that he'd stop by to see you sometime next week."

It was a glorious spring day. The sun was warm, the breeze gentle, sweet with the scent of mixed blossoms in full bloom.

Stacy's mood bordered on euphoric, not unlike a child unexpectedly let out early from the chalk-cloaked schoolroom. She loved every inch of the farm, but the past months had been so traumatic, so fraught with grief and worry, and so very physically arduous for her, that the respite was as appreciated as it was sorely needed.

Freedom. It was wonderful. Life bubbled through Stacy, kissing her lips with an expectant smile, lighting her eyes from within with a brilliant sparkle.

Stacy's shimmering inner glow did not go unnoticed by her companion.

Lord, Stacy was beautiful.

Main startled himself with the sudden realization. From the first instant, he had thought her attractive, animated, appealing and sexy as all get out. But beautiful? Hardly. Yet illuminated from inside with happiness, and blessed on the outside with sunlight, Stacy was not merely beautiful but also a sight to behold.

Looking at her made him feel good...psychologically. Physically, observing her made him hurt. It was a welcome ache, one Main had not experienced to any strong degree for well over a year. He savored the sensation, while despairing the discomfort of clawing urgency and frustration.

A dilemma, for certain. But one Main could contend with, given the hope of surcease in the foreseeable future. For the moment, he was content to bask in the mind- and body-warming glow of Stacy in springtime.

They set off in Stacy's five-year-old, racy-looking lipstick-red Camaro, she laughing at his groans about the probability of leg cramps from enforced confinement.

She made a quick run to Intercourse, then Bird-in-Hand, giving Main a slow drive-by look at the quiet rural communities, which came to bustling life with the onslaught of the summer tourist interest.

From Bird-in-Hand, Stacy headed for Ephrata, where she parked the car at the religious commune Cloister, established by Conrad Beissel in 1732.

"How many buildings are there?" Main asked with interest, grateful to stretch his legs as he strolled beside her.

"There are 20," Stacy answered, referring to the brochure she'd picked up at the visitor's center. "It says here that most of them are original, and trace the lifestyle of the residents of the period. The religious society disbanded in 1814."

"Life was surely easier then," he observed, with tongue obviously in cheek.

Stacy sensed the hook, but rose obligingly to the bait anyway. "Why?"

"No small cars to fold themselves into."

From the Cloister, they made a quick tour of the Ephrata Museum, then crawled back into the vehicle Main had dubbed "the torture chamber" for the run to Lititz.

Since Main was echoing the noises issuing from his empty stomach, Stacy parked the car in a lot across the street from the Candy Americana Museum and Candy Outlet at the Wilbur Chocolate Company factory. Main eyed the building speculatively as he eased his long legs from the car.

"You're suggesting chocolate for lunch?"

"You don't like chocolate?" Stacy managed a wide-eyed, innocent expression.

"Yeah, I like chocolate," he retorted, turning a frown on her. "But not necessarily for lunch."

"Okay." With a shrug, and a grin, she pocketed her car keys and flickered her fingers in a beckoning gesture as she sauntered by him. "Then we'll walk down this street to the intersection of Main, and have lunch at General Sutter Inn."

"An inn?" Main was beside her in two long, muscle-stretching strides. "With food?"

"Very good food," she promised, laughing outright as she broke into a trot to keep up with him. "It was erected somewhere around 1760 or 1770, and originally named Zum Anker."

"Zum Anker?" They reached the intersection and as. they waited for the light to change, Main examined the exterior of the structure situated on the opposite corner. "Why?"

"Beats me." Stacy moved her shoulders in a help-less shrug. "Maybe that was the name of the man who had it built."

"Some tour guide you are." Muttering about her dearth of historical information, Main shepherded her across the street and into the deep veranda wrapped around the corner of the building. "If the food isn't good, sweetheart, you're in trouble."

The place was a period piece. The servers, attired to complement the decor, were friendly and efficient. Fortunately, for Stacy, the food wasn't just good, it was first-rate. But then, she knew it would be; she'd eaten there before.

The inner man fed and content, Stacy tugged the outer man away from his perusal of a selection of brochures of local points of interest, and back onto the street.

"That big place over there—" She inclined her head to indicate a lovely old home set across the intersecting street. "That's the John Augustus Sutter House. He had it built around 1870, at a cost of $10,000."

"Sutter," Main murmured, frowning. "Why do I feel I should recognize that name?"

"California?"

"Sutter's Mill!" he exclaimed. "The gold fields."

"Go to the head of the class." Stacy gave another tug on his hand to get him moving. "Now, how about a stroll along Main Street—" she shot a grin at him "—Main?"

The town was obviously old, quaint, quiet and attractive. Many of the buildings set close to the tree-lined sidewalk were dated as well as named.

"Lititz," Main said aloud, reading from a brochure he had picked up at the inn. "Did you know the town was named for a community in Bohemia?"

"Yes," Stacy nodded. "By Moravians."

"Yeah. Hey, how about this?" he said, still reading. "First they established a school in 1746, and then a church in 1749. They laid out the town in 1756, and only Moravians were permitted to live here for the first one hundred years."

"How about that."

"Incredible."

"That only Moravians were permitted to live here until the 1850s?"

"No." Main shook his head. "The age of the place. The residents in many parts of Texas think a place is old if it dates back one hundred years. This place goes back to 1746."

"Lancaster goes back to 1729."

"No sh—uh, kidding?" Main glanced away from the brochure with a look of keen interest.

"No kidding."

"Let's go."

His unconcealed eagerness brought a smile to her lips. "After the chocolate factory. I want dessert."

They both munched Wilbur Buds during the short drive from Lititz to Lancaster. In between popping the sweet dark chocolate morsels into his mouth, Main serenaded Stacy in a deep, attractive, singsong voice.

"Oh, I be a ramblin', ah...*r-a-m-b-l-i-n*...apostrophe..."

* * *

"Well, I guess we've kinda done Lancaster," Main said some hours later, slanting a grin at Stacy.

Boy, had they done Lancaster! Stacy agreed in silent weariness, grinning back at him. They had trekked all over the place, hitting all the pertinent sights of interest. Beginning with the city's focal point at the Soldiers and Sailors Monument in Penn Square at the intersecting streets of King and Queen. They inspected the works of quilts, woodenware, clocks, long rifles and other items fashioned by Lancaster County craftsmen displayed in the Heritage Center Museum of Lancaster, which was the old City Hall building.

From the Museum, they'd moved on to the Central Market, then through Steinman Park to the Steinman Hardware Company, founded in 1744.

"The store closed its doors in 1965," Stacy had said, reading from a guidebook Main had purchased. "Till then, it was the oldest continuously operating hardware store in these United States."

"Fascinating," Main had commented, sounding like he really meant it.

They'd stopped to read a historic marker at the birth site of Major General John Reynolds, who was killed on the first day of the Battle of Gettysburg.

"I want to go to Gettysburg, too."

Stacy had thrown him a stern look. "Not today."

"Tomorrow?" Main had asked hopefully.

"If we get through today."

They'd walked for over an hour, then had stopped for a cold drink before returning to the car. Now, declaring their next stop the last of the day for her, Stacy drove to Wheatland, the Federal-style house that was the home of President James Buchanan from 1848 until his death in 1868.

Heading back to the car some forty minutes later, Main draped an arm around Stacy's shoulders, confessing, "This ramblin' Texan be tired. I be ready to go home."

"And not a moment too soon," Stacy groaned, laughing at him. "This Pennsylvanian not be tired. This Pennsylvanian be damn near dead."

After departing Wheatland, they made one more stop, on Main's insistence, and without a peep of protest from Stacy, for dinner at a restaurant on the outskirts of Lancaster.

Revived by a hearty, traditional Pennsylvania Dutch meal of pork and sauerkraut with mashed potatoes and milky buttered dried lima beans on the side, Stacy and Main returned home, to face the chore of mucking the stables and bringing in the horses.

"I can't believe you do this alone every weekend," Main said, trailing her into the house when the work was done.

"Believe it," Stacy muttered, stifling a yawn.

"We're going to have to talk about hiring some help," he went on doggedly, following her to the stairway.

"Not now," Stacy said determinedly, mounting the stairs. "I'm for the shower, and then bed."

"When, then?" Main called after her.

"Tomorrow...maybe."

"In Gettysburg?"

Stacy gave a loud, exaggerated groan.

Main laughed.

Sunday, they did Gettysburg.

After another surprisingly restful night, Stacy woke early, but still not early enough to beat Main into the kitchen. She found him at the table, coffee mug in hand, reading the Sunday paper.

"Good morning." Main glanced away from the newsprint to smile at her. "Rested?"

"Morning," she murmured, heading for the coffee-pot. "And yes. Are you?"

"Rarin' to go."

"Umm." Stacy rolled her eyes. "The chores have to be done first, you know."

"I'm hip." He grinned. "You want to eat now, or get the work out of the way and have breakfast on the road?"

Enthusiasm rose in Stacy. "I'd love to eat breakfast I didn't have to cook. Let me gulp down this coffee. Then I'll be ready to work."

Main deserted all the news fit to print. "I'll chase the animals out of the stables." He paused in the door-way. "How long will it take to get to Gettysburg?"

"Stopping for breakfast..." she said, swallowing the last drops of coffee. "About an hour and a half, give or take."

They hit the highway less than two hours later. The weather cooperated by being almost summer balmy. They dawdled over huge breakfasts and second cups of coffee. The trip to the famous battlefield took closer to two hours.

Stacy and Main conversed in low murmurs while strolling about the respectfully hushed environs of Gettysburg. He gave her a brief and expurgated account of his sojourn in New York City, followed by his less stressful stay in West Texas. In exchange, she filled in for him more details about her own life, with her parents, her brother and her beloved grandfather.

"And, so you see, I always believed the farm was to come to me," she concluded, offering him a smile. "That's why I was so upset when I learned about you."

"Understandable." Main returned the smile. "Are you now resigned to sharing it with me?"

Stacy's smile faded. "Yes."

"And the rest of your life?" Main asked, probing further. "Are you ready to commit to sharing that with me, too?"

It was only then, when Stacy began to feel pressured, that she realized that Main had been biding his time, giving her thinking space, while surrounding her with the pleasure derived by his companionship, his laconic humor, and most weakening of all, his laughter.

"I'm leaving tomorrow morning," he reminded her.

Stacy sighed. Despite what she previously believed, she knew she would miss him. "I know, but . . ."

"You need more time?"

"Yes, please." Stacy looked away.

Main caught her by the chin, turning her to face him again. "Will you have a decision for me when I return?"

She hesitated, then nodded. "Yes."

Although his smile was gentle, a devilish light glittered in the depths of Main's gray eyes.

"It had better be yes."

Main was gone—back to West Texas.

Stacy awoke Monday morning to a house that seemed empty, too quiet, devoid of life.

Had he really only been in the house for such a short time? Stacy marveled, tossing back the bedcovers. Main had been there three days, and not even three full days at that.

Incredible, Stacy mused, sitting on the edge of her bed. Just three short days, and now the house seemed desolate, deserted, abandoned.

The house . . . and Stacy.

She missed the sound of his laughter.

A soft, reminiscent smile curved Stacy's lips. Main's spontaneous laughter had rung out often over the past three days. It was a joyous sound, infectious, deep, rich with the flavor of his quick humor. And revealing of the person.

Jasper Chance was a man at peace with himself.

Stacy Hunsberger was the one in turmoil.

A sigh whispered past Stacy's guard. She had yet to make a decision concerning Main's unorthodox proposal. True to his word, he had not badgered her. Instead, he had been of inestimable assistance to her with the daily, and seemingly, never-ending chores, thus freeing more of her time for more pleasurable pursuits.

The smile sprang back to her lips. Opposed to what she would have previously believed, they had had fun together.

# Twelve

*She was going to marry him.*

Stacy wasn't sure exactly when the decision settled in her mind. All she knew was, nearly a week to the day he had arrived on the scene, suddenly and without warning, she knew she was going to say yes to Main's proposal.

In truth, she had relatively little choice in the matter... not if she wanted to keep the farm intact. She needed money; Main had money. But he had made his position crystal clear. Main had no intentions of being a distant, silent partner. He would be a part of it all, on site, living it, working it, or a part of none of it.

And, for Stacy, the bottom line was, she had nothing to offer him, no inducement, other than herself. In the end, it came down to either or—her freedom or the farm. Throughout that week, Stacy had thought of little else.

And it wasn't even that she had had nothing else to occupy her hands or mind. Stacy had had her mind and hands full with the everyday work on the farm, in addition to keeping Dan and Anne from flying at each other's throats, teeth and claws bared for damage-inflicting combat.

At least, Stacy had thought Dan and Anne were swiftly approaching open warfare.

Silly her.

Later, in retrospect, considering how, and how quickly, events progressed, Stacy could only surmise that she was existing in a state of major distraction at the time.

In the end, late Thursday afternoon, Dan and Anne did fly at each other. No serious wounds were dealt from either side—except of the emotional variety.

Dan had come to the farm after lunch, in response to a call from Stacy concerning what appeared to be a pulled ligament in the left hind leg of one of the mares.

"So, the Texan's gone?" Dan said, meeting Stacy halfway along the path from the house to the stables.

"Yes," Stacy replied, reaching out to take his extended hand. "He left early Monday morning."

"Told me that was when he was planning to go." Dan squeezed her hand and smiled. "Any idea when he'll be back?"

Stacy shook her head negatively in answer.

"But he will be back?" he prompted.

"Yes." Stacy concealed a sigh beneath a smile. "He will be back."

Dan slanted a sharp-eyed, pensive look at her. "You all right, Stace? I mean, did everything go all right while he was here? He didn't hassle you or anything?"

"No, he didn't hassle me." Stacy slid a sidelong glance at him, weighing the pros and cons of confiding in him. Dan just might agree with her decision to accept Main's archaic proposition. Then again, he just might tell her that she was out of her tiny little mind.

"Something's gnawing at you, Stace." Dan stopped walking and turned to peer into her face. "I'm here, and on your side, if you need somebody to talk to."

Stacy hesitated a moment longer, feeling foolish, gullible and light years from certain that she had chosen the right course of action. Main's solution to their problem might not be as aboveboard and as mutually beneficial as he made it sound. There could be hidden pitfalls for her, even if she couldn't think of any at the present moment.

Main had appeared so straightforward, so sincere. But, appearance and reality were quite often two entirely different things.

He laughed a lot.

But was he laughing with her... or at her?

Stacy bit her lip. Hard.

"Stace?" Real concern edged Dan's voice. "I knew it. There is something." Anger crept into his tone. "Out with it," he ordered, sounding like her brother, and even more like her father. "What did he do?"

"He asked me to marry him." There. It was said. Out in the open. Stacy held her breath, waiting for his reaction. She didn't have to wait long.

"He did what!" Dan's expression went blank, then was washed by sheer incredulity.

"He proposed a marriage of mutual convenience."

Dan stared at her, looking like he had been pole-axed. "Well, go on. Don't leave it there. What did you say? How did you answer him?"

"I didn't." She shrugged. "I told him I needed time to think about it."

"I should hope so." Something—her obvious nervousness, her evasive eyes—alerted him. "You've made a decision," he said, perceptively. "Haven't you?"

"Yes." Stacy swallowed, then went on in a rush, "I'm going to accept his proposal."

Dan merely stared at her, nonplussed, for long seconds. "Are you sure this is what you want?"

Stacy bit back the quick "no" that sprang to her tongue. Was she a grown woman or a scared little girl, needing reassurance from big brother?

"Yes." The strength in her voice was mirrored in the challenging tilt of her chin. "I'm sure."

"My, my," Dan murmured. A teasing gleam sparkled in his eyes. "Is this the same Stacy Hunsberger who swore never to enter into the bondage of matrimony?"

Stacy gave a superior sniff. "But that's the beauty of the thing, you see. We're not talking about a gooey love match here, in which the woman vows to love, honor and *obey* ... and the man takes it as his due that she comply."

"We're talking about a marriage of convenience," Dan reminded her in a dry drawl. "A convenient husband."

Convenient husband. Stacy's mind was flooded with an image of Main—his gray eyes darkened by passion, his voice soft, his body hard, his mouth . . .

Go away! Banishing the vision with a sharp head shake, Stacy smiled with calculated condescension. "We're talking about a legal union entailing mutual trust, respect and an equal sharing of responsibilities."

"And do you trust and respect him?"

Caught off guard by Dan's perceptive question, Stacy gazed at him in consternation, while she swiftly sorted through her feelings regarding Main.

Did she trust and respect him?

She hardly knew him.

How could she tell? By what yardstick could she measure the length of her possible trust and respect?

Her feelings swirled, then spun out the answer in the echoing sound of Main's voice.

*But should you decide to enter into this agreement, you can be certain of one thing. I will never give you a moment of doubt about my fidelity. I give you my word here and now that I will honor the conditions of the agreement and my marriage vows until the day I die.*

But had she believed him?

Yes.

"Yes, I do," Stacy finally replied in an adamant tone of firm conviction.

"So, it would seem your grandfather chose the right coheir for you." He chuckled. "He gets his way . . . however inadvertently."

"Well, not all that inadvertently." Stacy's smile was faint, bittersweet.

"What do you mean?"

Briefly and concisely, Stacy recounted the story her lawyer had told her about her grandfather and his stepsister. "And so," she finished, "Gramps was keeping everything in the family...in a way."

Dan stared at her in amazement for a moment, then he laughed and shook his head. "That's kinky."

"Isn't life?"

"Too true," Dan agreed, then grimaced and glanced around. "Talking about kinky...where's the young groom?"

Stacy sighed and frowned. "Dan, please. I've got enough on my mind. Don't start on Anne."

"She's a menace."

"She's doing a good job!"

He snorted and strode off toward the stables. "I hope you didn't let her near the mare's injured leg."

"Dan, I mean it!" Stacy warned, hurrying after him. "I don't want you upsetting her."

"Which one...the mare or Anne?" he shot back, lengthening his stride.

"Damn it, Dan!" she yelled, breaking into a trot.

He was loping past the tack room at the end of the stables, and with a wave of his hand, called back, "The phone in the tack room is ringing."

"Oh, nuts." Stacy hesitated, tempted to ignore the blasted thing, then, muttering to herself, she veered off in the direction of the tack room door.

"Hello?" Her voice was rough, breathless, less than welcoming and polite, as she barked into the receiver.

"Dammit, woman, get away from that horse!"

Stacy winced at the angry sound of Dan's voice, and she craned her neck to peer through the small window in the tack room door.

"Miss Hunsberger?"

She frowned at the receiver she had forgotten she was holding. "Yes. Who's calling?"

"I was following Stacy's instructions!" Anne shouted, distracting Stacy.

"This is Calvin Muntz from the feed store" came the voice on the phone, vying for her attention. "The order you called in this morning is ready. You can pick it up anytime."

"Oh, uh . . . okay, I'll—"

"I'll take care of her." Dan's harsh tone intruded. "Go—find something else to do."

"Miss Hunsberger?"

"And you can go to—"

"Yes!" Stacy exclaimed, drowning out the rest of Anne's advice to Dan. "I'll pick it up later this afternoon."

"I swear, girl, if you . . ." Dan was saying, again snagging Stacy's attention.

What *was* going on in there? Dan sounded on the point of violence! She had to get in there and break it up before they came to blows.

"Anytime, ma'am."

"Huh?" Stacy frowned at the phone.

"Your order, ma'am," Calvin explained, slowly and carefully. "It will be ready."

"Oh! Thank you. I—" Stacy broke off as a crash sounded from inside the stables. Good heavens!

"Ah...yes, thank you. This afternoon. Goodbye."
Slamming the receiver onto the cradle, she made a
beeline for the connecting door.

The doorknob resisted her fumbling effort to turn it.
Fear clutched at Stacy's throat. Since the crash, a ter-
rifying silence had descended in the stable.

Surely Dan had not struck Anne!

The thought lent impetus to Stacy's actions. The
knob turned. The door swung open. She dashed into
the stable and along the long row of stalls.

God! If Dan had hurt Anne—

Stacy's thoughts and forward motion came to a
screeching halt as she approached the lame mare's stall.

There, standing alongside the docile animal, Dan
held Anne in a crushing embrace.

What in the name of hell did the man think he was
doing? Stacy protested in silent outrage. Was he trying
to break Anne's spine?

On closer inspection, Stacy was suddenly hit with the
realization that Dan apparently knew precisely what he
was doing—and that Anne was actively helping him do
it.

And what they were doing—together—was kissing.
No. Dan and Anne were not merely kissing. They were
devouring one another...with their mouths and their
hands.

Eyes wide, mouth agape, Stacy stared at the couple,
too stunned to do anything more than stare.

Anne's fingers twined through Dan's hair, tugging
with frantic insistence, not to tear him away from her,
but to pull him closer to her parted, searching lips.

Dan's hands moved with restless urgency, over Anne's shoulders, her back, her hips, where they grasped, drawing her slender body up, into hard contact with his.

Holy leaping Hanna!

Stacy watched them, unable to tear her riveted gaze away, while her stunned senses quivered from the memory of being aroused in a similar manner. The scene blurred before her eyes as she relived the moments spent in a similar embrace, being crushed and caressed by Main.

Stacy felt a flutter in her chest, and a melting heat lower in her body. She could smell him, feel him, taste him. And the taste of him made her hungry for more.

She ached. Lord, how she ached. She wanted... wanted...

Main.

The yearning admission startled Stacy from her erotic reverie. She blinked, clearing away the heat haze. Dan and Anne were still pressed together, oblivious of her, and of their surroundings.

With her mental faculties back in working order, Stacy saw the mare tilt her large head to look at the preoccupied couple askance. The mare's nostrils flared; her big eyes rolled, and she moved her rump in warning.

She had to get them out of there, before the mare took it into her head to give them a nudge... and flatten the two of them against the side of the stall, however innocently.

"Dan!" Stacy called sharply. "Anne! Will you two come up for air? You're beginning to make the mare, and me, nervous."

Dan ended the kiss with slow, obvious reluctance. He glanced around, as though getting his bearings, then carefully backed Anne from the stall, to safety.

Anne was flushed, her eyes luminous, her lips moist and full with a thoroughly kissed look.

"I heard a crash," Stacy said, breaking into their absorption with each other.

They were now away from the confines of the stall, out of harm's way, but still Dan kept Anne close, safe within the encircling band of one arm.

"Dan lined the water bucket at the wall," Anne explained, sliding a sultry-eyed gaze at the vet.

"Dan did what?" Stacy stared at him in sheer disbelief; she couldn't remember any occasion when Dan gave vent to his feelings with violent action.

"I was mad...at Anne." His smile was wry, and self-deprecating. "I think I had about reached the end of my tether. I had to do something."

"But you kissed her!"

"I wanted to shut her up." Dan's smile curved with smug satisfaction. "It was either kiss her or strangle her." He ran a fiery gaze over Anne's flushed face, ending with her kiss-pursed lips. "This kiss worked."

"Miracles," Anne murmured, caressing him with a misty-eyed gaze.

The muscles in Dan's arm flexed convulsively, and he hauled Anne hard against him. The heat of embarrassment flared in Stacy as she watched him lower his head to the younger woman.

"I think this is about where I came in," she repeated Dan's words of a week ago. Feeling decidedly de trop, like a third wheel on a bicycle, she edged away from the distracted couple. "Uh ... I have to pick up the order at the feed store."

Noting that neither of the two was paying the slightest interest to her, Stacy shrugged. "Well, I thought they hated each other," she said in passing to her pet as she loped past Morning Star's stall. "So go figure."

Throughout the following week, Dan found all number of reasons to visit the farm—most of them suspicious, some downright funny. Except, by then, Stacy was in no mood to do much laughing.

She hadn't heard as much as a word from Main, and time and absence were beginning to do a job on her nerves and emotional system.

The image of Dan and Anne, locked together in a passionate embrace, was impressed on the forefront of her mind, with one difference. In Stacy's image, the fervent participants were she and Main, not Dan and Anne.

Her blood flowed, hot and eager.

She wanted him.

Had Main changed his mind?

The fearful thought kept Stacy fidgety by day and sleepless by night.

By the end of the second week, hardly able to deal with her own thoughts, never mind her unusual feelings, Stacy was pale, edgy and short-tempered. Both

Dan and Anne were giving her a wary eye and a wide berth.

"Hello?" Stacy snarled into the receiver upon answering the ringing phone late Sunday night.

"Did I wake you?"

The low warm sound of Main's voice melted Stacy's temper. And her bones. Did he wake her? She asked herself. God, yes! He had wakened every living, clammering cell in her body!

"No, I was working on the books," Stacy replied, making a sour face at the ledger open on the desk.

He laughed.

She shivered.

"Do they balance?"

Stacy sighed. "No."

"They will." Main's voice conveyed absolute certainty. "Starting next week."

Stacy was afraid to ask, but she had to know. "You...uh, you're coming back?"

"Yes." Main hesitated. Then his voice even lower, somewhat rough, he said, "Are you going to marry me?"

This was it. The moment—her moment—of truth. Stacy drew a deep breath, and then another.

"Stacy?" Main demanded a response.

"Yes."

# Thirteen

---

Main was back.

The deed was done.

They were married.

Stacy was scared.

Pacing the length of her bedroom, nervously twisting the narrow gold band on her left ring finger, Stacy shot apprehensive glances at the door, while attempting to shoot grit into her weakening spine by talking to herself like a Dutch uncle. So far, the only thing she had derived from the exercise was a heavy tiredness in her legs.

And it wasn't even as though she were a virgin, or anything, Stacy chided herself, jerking upright at a whispery noise. She soughed through her dry lips when she realized that the noise had emanated from the wind-rustled leaves on the tree outside her bedroom window.

Although it was true that the occasion of her one and only foray into the realm of the senses and sensuality had been fraught with a twinge of pain and over-whelming disappointment, she was, in actual fact, no longer a virgin... at least not physically. Emotionally, Stacy could be likened to the proverbial driven snow.

At the time of her initiation, Stacy's erstwhile, inept lover had been an inexperienced college boy.

Jasper Chance was most definitely a man; a man, moreover, with unusual depth and sensitivity, as he had proved to her on the very day he had returned to the farm.

Stacy's thoughts and emotions quivered in remem-brance of that day two weeks ago....

Main had driven onto the property towing a U-Haul behind a high, travel-begrimed four-wheel-drive vehi-cle. Stacy had not been surprised to hear Main con-firm that everything of value he owned was stowed in the piled-high trailer. He had come to stay. In his mind, he was home.

But Stacy had been surprised a short time later when, seated opposite him at the kitchen table, Main had slid a bulging manila envelope across the table to her.

"What is this?" she'd asked, frowning.

"Two gifts," he'd replied. "One from me, and one from my grandmother. Open it."

A gift from him... and his grandmother! Stacy had quivered with equal sensations of curiosity and excite-ment. Fumbling with the metal clasps, she opened the envelope flap and withdrew a thick sheaf of papers, paper-clipped in two separate bunches. It was immediately obvious to Stacy that the top bunch was Main's gift to her. An unusual but insightful and thoughtful gift, indeed.

The crisp sheaf of papers clipped together were all medical reports, both from private physicians and medical laboratories, attesting to the excellent health of one Jasper Chance.

Both stunned and touched by the magnitude of his consideration for her, Stacy had glanced up from the papers to stare into his watchful eyes.

"This...this wasn't necessary," she said, in an emotion-strained voice.

"I know." Main shrugged. "But I wanted you to feel safe." A smile curved his mouth and lightened the gray of his eyes. "Now look at your other gift."

Forewarned of a further shock, Stacy turned her attention to the second sheaf of papers. There were four sheets in all, comprising a letter to her from Main's grandmother—Stacy's grandfather's beloved stepsister. Trembling, Stacy began to read the delicate handwriting.

My dear Stacy,
Welcome to the family. You cannot possibly imagine the sense of satisfaction and joy it gives me to write these words to you at long last. Your grandfather was the only brother I ever had...or wanted. I loved him. And I now happily extend that love to you....

Tears rushed into Stacy's eyes, blurring her vision. She raised her head to gaze at Main in mute appeal.

"You can finish reading the letter later," he said in understanding. "I'll give you the gist of the contents."

Main drew a breath, then launched into a brief, concise report of his private meeting with his grandmother during the time he had spent in Tyler.

"I told her everything," he said. "About my surprise on being informed that I had been named as co-heir in your grandfather's will, about the farm, and about you ... and my subsequent proposal of marriage." His lips tilted into a wry smile. "She already knew, and confessed as much."

Stacy blinked. "She knew?"

"Mmm." Main nodded. "Appears she called him, sometime last summer." He chuckled. "Her exact words were, 'after missing him for all these long years, and enduring his stubborn silence, I just picked up the phone, got the number from Information and called the stiff-necked old fool.'"

The description was so accurate, Stacy had to laugh.

Main laughed with her. "Yeah. Anyway, she said they talked for over three hours. He told her all about you, but more to the point, our point, she told him all about me." He arched his dark brows. "Apparently, your grandfather liked what he heard, and that's when he conceived the idea of leaving me a half interest in the farm. From her account, he knew that I could help you financially."

The mystery was solved. At least, as solved as Stacy figured it would ever be. She hadn't bothered to tell

Main the conclusion she and Dan had reached concerning her grandfather's motives. It no longer mattered.

In the interval before the wedding, Stacy had read the letter from Main's grandmother numerous times, and had decided the now-elderly woman was quite a lady.

And the lady's grandson was quite a man.

The man scared the hell out of her.

Coward. Jellyfish. Spineless ditz. Stacy raked her mind for more chastising appellations to apply to herself in hopes of bracing her flagging courage.

Her mind emptied, only to be filled the next instant with an image of her new, convenient husband as he had appeared that afternoon—their wedding afternoon.

Main was a feminine breath-catcher dressed in jeans or casual slacks and shirt; attired in a dark three-piece suit, pristine white shirt and a natty tie, he presented a vivid picture of walking female devastation.

In a word, Stacy had been stunned.

To give the devastator his just due, Main had orchestrated the ceremony, Stacy, himself and all others concerned, with the finesse of a much-vaunted maestro.

On his suggestion, he and Stacy had left the farm early that afternoon in separate vehicles, ten minutes apart, Main going first. Stacy had arrived at the small church she attended—on a fairly regular basis—to find Main, along with her pastor, Dan, and Anne, and Edith and her husband, waiting for her.

Main's expression of near awe when he saw her, dressed in a summer-flower-splashed, ankle-length frock of soft, whisper-thin cotton, merely added to Stacy's already advanced stage of jitters.

Concealing her nervousness behind a bright smile, and an even brighter greeting, Stacy had joined the group on the church walkway.

"Are we ready?" The elderly cleric asked, blessing the group with a beatific smile.

"I ... I suppose," Stacy had answered, in a croaking voice more suited to a frog pond.

"Yes, we *are* ready," Main had confirmed in a soft, adamant tone, reminiscent of Stacy's grade-school principal.

Both Dan and Anne had been content to offer nothing more than knowing grins, while Edith and George beamed their approval.

Following the somberly attired pastor, Main ushered Stacy into the quiet church, motioning for their two smug-faced attendants to keep up.

At a positioning gesture from the good reverend, they then arranged themselves before the two steps leading to the chancel. The pastor took his place on the top step.

Stacy drew a deep breath, then let out a muffled yelp as a loud chord was struck on the church organ. At the same time, she was forced to swallow a giggle, as she heard the unmistakable sound of a muttered imprecation from the irreverent man standing to her right side.

The church organist, a robust woman of indeterminate years, continued happily pounding away until, at last, she caught up to the end of "I Love You Truly."

The pastor cleared his throat.

Anne coughed.

Dan shuffled his feet.

Main flexed his fingers.

Stacy heard her stomach issue a nervous growl.

She wanted to die—or, at the very least, escape the scene with a Victorian swoon.

She did neither of those disruptive things. Instead, Stacy stood beside Main, listening to the pastor recite the traditional and beautiful ceremony of marriage. She heard Main's strong voice respond and, in turn, the sound of her own, weaker, tremulous tones of acceptance.

The enormity of the course she had taken hit Stacy when the pastor invited Main to kiss his bride.

Main's kiss was brief—a gentle brushing of mouth against mouth. It had the same effect as her first sight of him.

Stacy was stunned.

The condition proved beneficial, as it had enabled her to get through the flurry of congratulations at the church, and the subsequent dinner Main had arranged for the two of them and Dan and Anne at a quaint inn nearby.

She had conversed, hopefully with some intelligence, and had even laughed a time or two during the leisurely and extended meal, all the while dreading the coming night.

Stacy had found her tongue less glib when she and Main returned to the farm after parting company with the former antagonistic, but now disgustingly "together" and obviously "in-love" Dan and Anne.

She had become more quiet and withdrawn while they worked side by side completing the forever stable chores.

Though, later, Main had made an attempt at light conversation over coffee, Stacy had not been able to rise above the most mundane, monosyllabic responses, except when he mentioned the sudden change in Dan's and Anne's respective attitudes toward one another.

"I don't know what happened," she told him, still confused herself about the change in the couple. "One minute they were screaming at each other, and the very next thing I knew they were all over one another, in a clinch so intimate, I could almost feel the heat radiating from them."

Main's smile had held hints of amusement and satisfaction. "I knew it," he said, laughing softly. "I detected the scent of electricity between them from the first."

Stacy didn't particularly like hearing that; it made her feel unattentive, if not completely dense. "You could?" She frowned. "Strange...I really believed they disliked each other."

"The show of antagonism was pure self-defense," he said, smiling at her over the rim of his coffee cup. "In other words, they were both fighting a losing battle...and knew it." He shrugged. "It was just a matter of time and proximity."

*Proximity.* Stacy repeated the word to herself while measuring the table-width distance separating them. The night, with its attendant intimacies, loomed in her mind. Her throat went dry. Her mind went blank. She shut down.

Watching the play of emotions on her face, Main had made no comment on her renewed reserve, but merely suggested, sober-faced but with a suspicious gleam in his eyes, that it had been a long day, following a long two weeks, and that it was understandable if she felt tired.

Wrong. She had been wide-awake, alert and a quivering basket case.

And now, night had arrived—*the* night—bringing with its shrouding darkness a throat-parching skittishness as a wedding-night gift to the new Mrs. Chance.

Another whispery sound reached her. Stacy stopped pacing and whirled to glare at the window. Main tapped on the bedroom door.

"Yes," Stacy squeaked, whipping around. "Uh...I mean, come in. It's open."

Despairing of her pitiful lack of as much as a show of sophistication, Stacy stood, stiff and tremulous, watching the door as it slowly swung inward.

A three-piece dark suit? Pristine white shirt? Natty tie? Hah! In comparison to faded tight jeans clinging between bare feet and a broad expanse of naked chest, the near-formal attire was an unqualified second best.

The man wasn't devastating at all.

He was deadly.

Suddenly Stacy felt both overdressed in the lacy negligee Anne had given her before leaving yesterday afternoon, and overexposed by the revealing filmy garment.

"You're not afraid of me, Stacy," Main said, gliding a narrow look over her tight features. "Are you?"

"No!" Stacy denied, while unconsciously edging back, away from him.

A soft, gentle smile played over his too-attractive mouth. "I won't hurt you, you know," he murmured, stalking her with silent footsteps.

"I...I know," she said in a breathless burst, continuing to back away.

Main cocked one brow at a quizzical angle. "Then why are you running?"

"Running?" She squawked. "Who's running?"

The answer came, not from Main, but the solid feel of her spine making contact with the far wall.

"Ah, Stace." Main took the few steps required to bring him to within a foot of her. Raising his hand, he touched her cheek, then slowly slid his fingertips to her lips. "I don't know why you're trembling," he murmured, increasing her tremors by brushing her lips with his thumb, "when I'm the one who's scared."

"You?" Stacy stared at him in wide-eyed disbelief. "But why? I mean, I know that you're experienced and...well, why should you be scared?"

"Because I want you so much," he answered with simple honesty. "And I'm afraid you don't want me."

His admission of vulnerability caught her by such surprise, Stacy blurted out the truth without giving a thought or consideration for self-protection.

"But I do want you!" The instant the confession passed her lips, her hand flew up to seal them.

Too late. Main heard, and acted.

Taking one short step, he filled the space separating them and drew her into his arms. Her soft curves fit against his hard angles to perfection.

Murmuring words barely audible, yet fully comprehended by Stacy, he drew her away from the wall, and inexorably closer to the bed.

He didn't rush, or clutch, or pressure her. With infinite gentleness and care, Main cradled her face in his cupped hands and gazed into her wide, emotion-clouded eyes.

"You're not sorry?"

Stacy blinked. "Sorry? For what?"

"For taking the step that brought you to this minute," he murmured. "Here, with me."

"No." Stacy moved her head in a quick, negative shake. "I . . . I'm a little nervous," she admitted. "But not sorry."

"Good." Main's tone was deep, wealthy with relief. Dipping his head, he sensitized her lips with a slow, tantalizing brush of his mouth. "You were so quiet before." Another brush of his lips drew a low moan from her. "I was beginning to think . . ." His voice faded out as he slid his hands from her face, down the column of her throat, onto her shoulders and down her spine. "I was getting damn nervous."

Throughout the length of the journey of his hands, Stacy's flesh had responded with a quiver to the feather-light stroking glide of his fingers. Warmth rushed from each touch point to converge in a delicious ache in the center of her femininity, stealthily stealing the strength from her limbs and her vocal chords.

"I...I..." It was no use; her power of speech abdicated to the strength of her feelings.

"Say it again, sweetheart," Main urged, sending a lightning bolt of sensation through her with the touch of his tongue to the corner of her mouth.

"Say...say..." Stacy could barely manage the words. "What do you want me to say?"

His tongue outlined her lower lip with fire. "That word. *Want.* Say it again. Tell me you want me."

She was on fire, blazing inside, consumed by a need rapidly growing out of control. She was too hot, too hot in the flimsy negligee. It felt like wool—heavy and scratchy. Drawing harsh, uneven breaths, she gasped out, "I want you. Main, please. I hurt with the wanting."

His eyes closed. She saw him swallow. When he opened his eyes they were as dark and stormy as thunderhead clouds, pierced by lightning streaks of passion.

"We're going to be so good together...so good." Drawing deep, shuddering breaths, Main brought his hands to the front of her negligee. "I need to touch you," he murmured in an emotion-tossed, ragged-sounding tone. "I need to feel you, naked, against me." As he spoke, his hands smoothed the gown from her trembling form. It floated to the floor, into a shimmering white pool at her feet.

His clasp light on her shoulders, Main drew his head back to look at her. A flame sparked in his eyes as his gaze slowly descended from her face to her tip-tilted breasts, to her nipped-in waist and then lower, to the mound of her womanhood.

"You are beautiful," he whispered, in a tone tinged with a note of genuine awe. "Every inch of you."

The heat of embarrassment flushed the surface of her skin. Never in her life had she stood so exposed and vulnerable before a man's eyes and judgment. Her gaze shied away from the blaze flaring in the depths of his eyes, bouncing off his hair matted chest to come to an abrupt halt on the snap closing of his jeans. The sight of the male fullness below the snap rattled her aroused senses—and loosened her unguarded tongue.

"One of... one of us is terribly overdressed," she blurted out, gulping as the fullness of him grew before her startled, wide-eyed gaze.

A chuckle rumbled from deep inside his chest and erupted in soft laughter from his mouth. "Only you could make me laugh at a moment like this," Main said, dropping his hands to the snap on his jeans. "Oh, yeah, sweetheart—" the snap flipped open; the zipper whirred "—we are going to be more than merely good together." The faded denim was pushed down, over narrow hips and long, muscular flanks.

Stacy's eyes widened even more. If Main had appeared devastating before—and he had—then unadorned, in full arousal, he was magnificent. Without conscious thought, she echoed him, word for word.

"You are beautiful. Every inch of you."

Main threw back his head, gave a veritable whoop of delighted laughter, then, sweeping her up into his arms, he literally dove with her onto the bed.

There ensued moments—long, sigh- and shiver-inducing moments of shared joyous laughter and low, intense murmurs of glorious discovery. With hands and fingertips, lips and tongue tips, they explored the contrasts of rough and smooth, soft and firm, hot and hotter.

Never, never had she imagined the earthshaking sensations to be derived from the glide of a masculine tongue over one quivering breast tip. Nor could she have envisioned the tremors set to quaking in the depths of her womanhood with the most gentle of probing touches of a man's long fingers.

Brought to vibrant life by long, hard kisses and soft, stroking caresses, Stacy was emboldened to feel the smoothness of Main's taut flesh with her seeking palms, taste the tantalizing saltiness of his warm skin, enfold the satiny fullness of him in her trembling hands.

Stacy was more than ready, more than eager, when at last Main slipped into position between her quivering thighs. He hesitated for a heartbeat, staring down, into her unafraid eyes, then he lowered his head. His mouth claimed hers at the exact instant he joined them together. With slow, deep strokes, his body merged with hers, creating an ever-upward spiral of tension, driving her wild, pushing himself, consummating their union, making it earthy and spiritual as well as legal.

Stacy slept, exhausted, in his arms. Her wildly tousled hair lay like a tangled curtain across his chest. Her palm domed his flat, masculine nipple.

Wide-awake, passion still simmering inside him, Main lightly stroked her silky thigh, breathed deeply of her delicate scent and aimed a bemused smile at the ceiling.

*Incredible.*

The thought tugged his smile into a grin. *Incredible* seemed insufficient a word to describe his feelings. Never, never before in his life had Main derived such intense pleasure and sheer satisfaction from the sharing of sensuality with a woman. And never before had he experienced the seemingly conflicting sensations of utter completion and unappeased hunger.

His wife. A receptive tremor skipped the length of Main's spine. Stacy was now his wife. His. In every meaning of the word. Stroking, stroking her soft flesh, Main closed his eyes and relived the thrill of being with his wife.

If Stacy was like silk on the surface, inside she was like warmed pulsating satin. And with his mouth, his tongue and his body, Main had plunged to the very depths of Stacy's satin, losing himself, his identity, inside her sweet warmth. Lost but not abandoned. For Stacy was with him, guiding him, being guided by him, giving, giving, even as she took, everything he was willing to give, which was everything.

Desire stirred, hard and painful.

Desire, and something else, something stronger, something more intangible, but more lasting.

Love.

*Incredible.*

Well, hell, why not? Main's smile tilted at a silly angle. Why the hell not? Gushy? Mushy? Gooey? You bet, Chance, he taunted himself. But there you have it. Like it or not. The thing of it was . . . Main liked it.

Now all he had to do was bring the light and laughter of his life around to the idea of liking it, too.

# Fourteen

Stacy had a problem.

The problem's name was Jasper Chance.

Stacy raised her arm and swept her gloved hand over her perspiration-beaded forehead. It was hot, humid—a normal day for mid-July.

Stacy didn't feel at all normal. She didn't feel like working, either. She felt like a fraud; she wasn't particularly crazy about the feeling. Admitting that her problem was self-created didn't help much.

After freely entering into a contractual agreement with Main, she knew she had had no moral right to go falling in love with him. But, right or not, that's what she'd done.

Stacy was helplessly, irrevocably, in love with her convenient husband.

For weeks, ever since their fantastic wedding night, when the realization of her love for him had broken over Stacy with the clarity of a brilliant spring dawn, she had longed to tell Main how she felt, pour her love over him like a cascading emotional waterfall.

But Main had made it crystal clear from the outset that love, romantic love, was the last thing he wanted.

The weeks spent containing her feelings were beginning to take a toll on Stacy. She felt burdened by her secret love, and yearned to share it as lavishly with him as they had shared everything else connected with their agreement.

But her love had never been a factor in their agreement. Stacy knew she had no right to make her burden Main's burden. She'd have to deal with it as best she could. And therein lay the root cause of her problem.

How long before she slipped up, gave herself away, revealing herself to Main as the fraud she was, and by doing so ruin the easygoing compatibility in the relationship they had formed over the preceding weeks?

The question was a constant thorn thrusting into Stacy's mind, interfering with her work, her life.

It would have to be resolved ... and soon. How that resolution might be achieved plagued Stacy at regular intervals, like that moment, when she really should be—

"Why don't you call it a day, Stace?" Main's call scattered her fruitless mental gyrations. "You've been putting Morning Star through her paces for hours," he finished, crossing the yard to the corral fence.

Collecting herself for the effect the sight of him always had on her composure, Stacy drew a deep breath and turned to look at him. Main was leaning against the top fence rail, smiling at her. The breath she had so carefully drawn rushed out with a soft whoosh.

It wasn't fair, Stacy cried in silent despair. Why did he have to look so good, *be* so good? And why had she gone and done something so dumb as fall in love with him?

"She's shaping up pretty nicely," she said, indicating the horse, and pushing her disturbing thoughts to the back of her mind. "Isn't she?"

"Better than that," Main agreed, running a quick glance over the animal. "She's going to make a beautiful and tough dressage competitor." He shifted his gaze to run a more lingering glance over Stacy. "And you look damned classy up there yourself, with your elegant seat on her back."

Stacy melted. Main noticed.

"There's something I want to discuss with you later," he said, determination steeling his tone.

"What?" Stacy asked with trepidation.

Main shook his head. "Later, after the help leaves for the day." He made to turn away, then paused to look back at her. "I have an errand to run, but I'll be back in plenty of time for dinner. We'll talk then."

No. We won't talk then. Stacy slowly shook her head as she watched him walk away from her. He was planning to confront her, accuse her of breaking their agreement by adding the pressure of her unwanted love to the deal. She wasn't prepared for that discussion. She had to think it through, find a way to explain, to tell him.

But not here.

Stacy skimmed a frantic glance around the area. Anne and the two men they had hired to help care for the animals—now doubled in number with the new horses they had recently purchased—were busy, and wouldn't notice or care if she left.

She needed time, but more importantly, she needed privacy. And she knew exactly where to find both.

The thought spurred her into action. Calling out to Anne to please stable Morning Star, Stacy took off for the house on the run. She'd leave a note for Main, of course, but she had to be by herself for a while, away from him, and the farm, which he had so quickly impressed with his personality.

"Stace?" Main called as the screen door banged shut behind him. The kitchen was empty; so was the stove. Not a single pot or pan sat atop the appliance, emitting mouth-watering aromas.

Frowning, he crossed to the back staircase. "Stace, you up there?" he shouted.

Silence. But more than silence. The place had an empty feel to it. The empty feel invaded Main's insides. He didn't appreciate the sensation; it made him uneasy.

"Of all times for her to go traipsing off somewhere," he grumbled, turning to walk to the table to deposit the results of his errand. The bottle of champagne landed on the tabletop with a soft thud. The tissue-wrapped red roses were laid with more care next to the bottle.

The best-laid plans...

"Damn!" Main exploded, striding again to the back stairs. He had planned every move he would make, every word he would say to her to convince her of how much he loved her, and to ask, plead, beg her if necessary, to try to love him back.

If his gut instincts were correct, and she was coming to care for him, as he'd been suspecting for some weeks now that she was, he wanted to look the part of the lover—not smell the part of a stable hand.

Telling himself that Stacy would be home soon, Main took the stairs two at a time. He'd have a shower while he waited for her, make himself presentable.

He exited from the bathroom twenty-odd minutes later, showered and shaved, his hair and teeth brushed to a sparkling gleam. He dumped his soiled clothes into the hamper, then strode along the hallway and into their bedroom, naked as a newborn, if not as innocent.

He went directly to the dresser for underwear and socks, and from there to the closet for slacks, shirt and shoes. He was working a foot into a soft-leather loafer when he thought he heard a noise outside in the yard.

"Stacy." Murmuring her name aloud, he strode to the window. A flash of white caught his eye as he passed the bed. Pausing in midstride, he turned to look. A scrap of white paper was pinned to the midnight-blue pillowcase.

A sensation too close to fear to be contemplated coiled through Main as he reached to unpin the note. His mouth tight, his features strained, he flipped open the folded sheet of lined notepaper and read the three tersely written sentences scrawled beneath his name.

Main,

I must get away for a while.

I need some space.

I must think.

"Damn!" Pivoting, Main strode from the room. He'd left it too late. "Fool," he accused himself, tearing along the hall and down the stairs. Back in the kitchen, he stood, irresolute. Every cell in his body cried out for action. But what sort of action could he take? He was still so new to the area, to Stacy.

Where had she gone? Where *could* she have gone? To Dan? To Anne? He shook his head. Stacy wouldn't carry her troubles to her friends. Her brother in California? Maybe. Sheer unreasoning panic clutched at his throat. What would he do if she decided not to come home?

Damn fool!

The brazen July sun surrendered the day with a fiery display along the horizon.

It would soon be dark, Stacy mused, jumping from her stone perch. It was time to go home. Absently brushing her palms over the seat of her jeans, she gazed at the city of Reading, spread out in the green valley from the base of the low mountain, upon which she had been sitting and thinking for some hours.

To be exact, Stacy hadn't been seated on the mountain itself, but on the stone wall bordering the scenic drive, aptly named Skyline Drive, that ran along the top of the mountain.

The alternating rows of yellow and red lights flickered to life on the building situated to her left, illuminating the Oriental upward curve of the tiered roofs of the landmark Reading Pagoda.

At Main's request, they had visited the city and the pagoda on the weekend after their wedding. They had driven along Skyline Drive, parked in the lay-by and sat on this exact spot on the wall to gaze at the city beneath and the hazy blue mountains in the distant west.

"It's a beautiful place," Main had murmured, unperturbed by the laughter and chatter of the many other tourists and local residents milling about. "A mind-soothing place. A thinking place."

The memory of his words had directed Stacy to the city, the scenic drive, the perch on the stone wall, to be alone, to remove herself from her husband's allure, to think.

Stacy's thoughts had centered on the events in her life since Main had first put in an appearance at the farm. She recalled the fear and resentment she had felt for him, and how quickly those debilitating emotions had changed to respect, admiration, trust and then love.

But there were other changes, too. The farm had seen its share. There was new hired help, new stock, new repairs made to the house and outbuildings. And not one of those changes had been wrought on the autocratic say-so of her convenient, and conveniently solvent, husband, although he had had the right to do so.

Main had discussed each and every one of those changes with Stacy, usually at the table over steaming cups of coffee, actively seeking her opinions and thoughts as to the distribution of his hard-earned, carefully invested fortune.

Was this the kind of man who would accuse her of fraud, of breaking their agreement, should he discover that she had fallen in love with him? Stacy had finally asked herself, as she watched the sun glide majestically into the horizon.

Of course not. The answer came swift and sure.

Then, what in summer blazes was she doing, sitting on a wall, however soothing, miles away from him?

It was with that question that Stacy jumped down from her hard stone perch.

Resolve firmed to conviction inside her as she drove toward home. She would tell Main the truth...and live with the consequences.

Main was waiting on the porch. Even in the brief flare of illuminating headlights, Stacy could see the tautness of his still body.

"Where in hell have you been?" he demanded, descending the porch steps as she pushed open the car door.

"For a drive," she answered, in a voice even she could hear was not quite steady. "I needed some—"

"Yeah, I know," his tight voice broke in. "You needed time, space...distance. From me?"

"Yes. No!" Stacy shook her head, preceding him up the steps and into the house.

"Well, what is it?" Main's voice took on a rough, ragged edge. "Yes or no?"

"Main, I..."

"Dammit, Stacy. Look at me!" Catching her by the wrist, he spun her around to face him. It was the nearest thing to an act of violence she had ever witnessed from him. His face looked drawn, pale. His eyes were dark, the dead gray of grief and loss. "Are you so unhappy with our arrangement?" He spoke each word as though it seared his tongue. "Do you want out?"

"Out?" Stacy's eyes flew wide. "No!" She swallowed. "Do...do you?"

"Me?" Main stared at her. "I didn't run away, leaving a damned note saying I needed time...and space." He snarled the last word. "Have I been crowding you?"

"No. Oh, no." Stacy shook her head, dislodging her hair clip and sending her hair swirling around her distraught face. "Main, believe me, I only wanted some private time." She wet her lips, and shivered when his gaze fastened on her mouth. "I had to think something through...alone."

He turned away, raked a hand through waves already ruffled by numerous rakings, then spun to face her again. "Why couldn't you think here? Maybe I could have helped you with your problem, whatever it is."

"You don't understand."

His laser stare bored into her. "So tell me."

"You're the problem."

Main turned to stone before her eyes. His cheeks, already pale, turned ashen. He closed his eyes, but too late to conceal the pain her blow had dealt him. "I see."

Stacy couldn't bear it. Couldn't endure the sight of him in pain, the stricken sound of his voice. No longer concerned with protecting herself, she ran to him, flinging herself against the solid strength of his body.

"No, no, Main, darling, you don't see!" Raising her hands, she captured his face in her palms. "I... I've cheated you, defaulted on our bargain."

"Did you call me darling?" A flame leapt in his eyes, only to be banked when he frowned. "Cheated me? How?" Before she could respond, his eyes narrowed. "Is there another man?"

"No!" Stacy exclaimed, spearing her fingers into his crisp hair. "Main, you asked me to swear my trust, honesty and fidelity to you, and I've honored that vow." She drew a shaky breath, then went on quickly, before she lost her nerve. "But you also told me you didn't want my love and..." Her nerve, and voice, failed in the crunch.

"And...?" The flare was back in his eyes, brighter, lighting the gray to shimmering silver. "Go on."

"I..." Stacy swallowed. "I..."

"If you don't say it," he said, in a low tone of warning. "I'll have to do something drastic."

"Drastic?" Excitement raced through Stacy— excitement, hope and thrilling anticipation. "Like... what?"

"Like this." In a reflection of her action, he brought his hands up to tangle his fingers in the silky strands of her hair, then lowered his head to capture her mouth.

After weeks of burning, mind-melting kisses, this one was a soul scorcher. Stacy felt like a cinder when he finally ended it, to an accompanying moan of protest from her, and raised his head to smile into her eyes.

"Say it."

"I love you."

"After that kiss you just curled my toes with—" his smile grew into a grin "—you had damn well better."

Stacy choked on a bubble of pure exhilaration charged laughter. "Do you... could you..."

"Be in love with you?" Main asked in a teasing, yet heart-stoppingly gentle tone.

"Could you?" Her voice was little more than a whispered plea of supplication.

The laughter fled from his eyes, replaced by a light of tenderness that stole her breath. "I could and I do. My own sweetheart, I have been in love with you, and falling more deeply in love with you, ever since the day I laid eyes on you."

A small, taunting smile curved Stacy's kiss flushed lips. "All romantic and gushy... huh?"

"Yes, all romantic and gushy," he confessed, color tingeing his cheeks as he turned her to face the table. "Champagne gushy and roses romantic... as you can see."

Tears stung Stacy's eyes. "Oh, Main," she whispered, moving away from him to stroke one deep red velvety petal with a trembling fingertip. "I must put them in water." She took a step, then exclaimed as he caught her to him and swung her off her feet, into his arms.

"Later," he murmured, striding to the back stairs. "The roses will keep... but I'm not so sure I will."

Looping her arms around his neck, Stacy snuggled into the enticing heat of him all the way to their bedroom, and even closer moments later, curving around him, as they lay together, unfettered by clothing, on the bed.

"I need to hear it again," Main murmured, driving her to the edge of madness with tiny bites, stinging kisses and the erotic play of his darting tongue.

"I... Oh! Don't stop!" Stacy cried, seeking the strength of him with her stroking hands. "I love you. I love you. I... Oh, Main! I love you so!"

Main sucked in a harsh breath when her hands captured him. "Stacy, Stacy. You can't know...you could never imagine how very much I love... Now you've done it." He pushed the words through gasping breaths. "Forgive me, sweetheart, but I can't wait. I must... I must..."

And he did—to Stacy's immeasurable delight.

Moonlight washed a swathe of silver across the top of the bed, casting into pale relief the serene features of the entwined lovers.

"That was not good." Main's tone held betraying laughter, robbing the sting from his observation.

"No?" Stacy squirmed around until she lay atop his chest, affording her the superior position from which she could scowl down at him. "Not good?"

"No." Main heaved a deep sigh of utter satisfaction and hugged her to him, crushing her breasts against his exertion slicked chest. "Not good. Wonderful. No." He shook his head. "Great. Not good enough, either." He frowned. "Marvelous. Fantastic. Fabu..."

"Are you telling me you enjoyed it?" Stacy laughingly interrupted him.

"It, and you, and our life, and..." He grinned. "I'm trying to tell you that I love you, and that I'm so happy I can hardly stand it."

Stacy's eyes and voice went soft. "All gushy and romantic, Mr. Jasper 'Main' Chance?"

The smile Main shot back at her was devil inspired.

"Chust so."

*   *   *   *   *

# SILHOUETTE® Desire™

## COMING NEXT MONTH

---

## AVAILABLE NOW:

# Take 4 bestselling love stories FREE

## Plus get a FREE surprise gift!

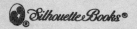